Cast of Chara‹

Gloria Rouston. She was as wealthy as ₅ₕₑ ₘₐₛ meek and unattractive. Did one of her gold-digging relatives try to kill her?

Jane Cowrer. The nom-de-plume Gloria uses after plastic surgeons transform her into a glamour girl.

Dick Rouston. Gloria's handsome and fun-loving husband. Money and women flow through his hands.

Sally Frame. Gloria's aunt. She met Dick through this aging beauty.

Rose Daly. Dick's widowed sister, who's dependent on Gloria for money.

Betsy Daly. Rose's daughter. She's a high school dropout, who's about to be shipped off to boarding school.

Pete Hoge. He fancies Rose—and does what she says. He also fancies Gloria's money.

Mamie Cowrer. She took Gloria in after she was pushed from a bridge. She's a good-hearted soul, if somewhat meddlesome.

John Cowrer. Mamie's nephew, he's a slightly stuffy young lawyer with political ambitions who falls for Gloria and marries her, not knowing that she's already married to Dick.

Dolly. The Cowrers' current maid and former maid to the Roustons. She loves gossip and roadhouses.

Dr. Zentron. Gloria's doctor. He has his doubts about Gloria's "death."

Allison Ketria. Dick's fiancée. She's a blonde who knows what she wants and how to get it.

Mr. and Mrs. Ketria. Her parents.

Midge. Allison's aunt.

Chief Evinston. The town's top cop. He's more worried about his corns than solving crimes.

Townspeople. Lucy Singer, proprietor of the Forget-Me-Not Tea Shop; **Gert,** a waitress at the tea shop; **Bub,** the hotel manager, who's new in town, and **Gus**, a helpful cab driver.

Books by Constance & Gwenyth Little

The Grey Mist Murders (1938)*
Black-Headed Pins (1938)*
The Black Gloves (1939)*
Black Corridors (1940)*
The Black Paw (1941)*
The Black Shrouds (1941)*
The Black Thumb (1942)*
The Black Rustle (1943)*
The Black Honeymoon (1944)*
Great Black Kanba (1944)*
The Black Eye (1945)*
The Black Stocking (1946)*
The Black Goatee (1947)*
The Black Coat (1948)*
The Black Piano (1948)*
The Black Smith (1950)
The Black House (1950)
The Blackout (1951)
The Black Dream (1952)
The Black Curl (1953)
The Black Iris (1953)

*reprinted by the Rue Morgue Press
as of March 2004

The Black Piano

by
Constance & Gwenyth Little

Rue Morgue Press
Boulder / Lyons

Printed at Johnson Printing
Boulder, Colorado

The Rue Morgue Press
P.O. Box 4119
Boulder, CO 80306

PRINTED IN THE UNITED STATES OF AMERICA

About the Littles

Although all but one of their books had "black" in the title, the 21 mysteries of Constance (1899-1980) and Gwenyth (1903-1985) Little were far from somber affairs. The two Australian-born sisters from East Orange, New Jersey, were far more interested in coaxing chuckles than in inducing chills from their readers.

Indeed, after their first book, *The Grey Mist Murders*, appeared in 1938, Constance rebuked an interviewer for suggesting that their murders weren't realistic by saying, "Our murderers strangle. We have no sliced-up corpses in our books." However, as the books mounted, the Littles did go in for all sorts of gruesome murder methods—"horrible," was the way their own mother described them—which included the occasional sliced-up corpse.

But the murders were always off stage and tempered by comic scenes in which bodies and other objects, including swimming pools, were constantly disappearing and reappearing. The action took place in large old mansions, boarding houses, hospitals, hotels, or on trains or ocean liners, anywhere the Littles could gather together a large cast of eccentric characters, many of whom seemed to have escaped from a Kaufman play or a Capra movie. The typical Little heroine—each book was a stand-alone—often fell under suspicion herself and turned detective to keep the police from slapping the cuffs on. Whether she was a working woman or a spoiled little rich brat, she always spoke her mind, kept her rather sarcastic sense of humor, and got her man, both murderer and husband. But if marriage was in the offing, it was always on her terms and the vows were taken with more than a touch of cynicism. Love was grand, but it was even grander if the husband could either pitch in with the cooking and cleaning or was wealthy enough to hire household help.

The Littles wrote all their books in bed—"Chairs give one backaches," Gwenyth complained—with Constance providing detailed plot outlines while Gwenyth did the final drafts. Over the years that pattern changed somewhat, but Constance always insisted that Gwen "not mess up my clues." Those clues were everywhere, and the Littles made sure there were no loose ends. Seemingly irrelevant events were revealed to be of major significance in the final summation. The plots were often preposterous, a fact often recognized by both the Littles and their characters, all of whom seem to be winking at the reader, almost as if sharing a private joke. You just have to accept the fact that there are different natural laws in the wacky universe created by these sisters. There are no other mystery writers quite like them. At times, their books seem to be an odd collaboration between P.G. Wodehouse and Cornell Woolrich.

The present volume, *The Black Piano*, is far darker than any other Little novel. Although it presents one of their most inventive plots, there is little of that sparkling byplay between the girl and her would-be suitor that was so evident in all of their earlier books. One wonders if both sisters were actually fully participating in the project at this point, or if they thought the postwar world called for new directions in their writing. Earlier books had given some indication that they were willing to go down new roads in their writing, including a relatively successful experiment with multiple point of view in *The Black Goatee*.

The Littles published their two final novels, *The Black Curl* and *The Black Iris*, in 1953, and if they missed writing after that, they were at least able to devote more time to their real passion—traveling. The two made at least three trips around the world at a time when that would have been a major undertaking. For more information on the Littles and their books, see the introductions by Tom & Enid Schantz to The Rue Morgue Press editions of *The Black Gloves* and *The Black Honeymoon*.

CHAPTER 1

MOONLIGHT TOUCHED the waterfall with silver, but left the narrow rustic bridge that spanned it half in shadow. The night was very still, and there was no sound except the clear, cool splash of the water as it fell onto the rocks below.

Gloria sighed, and rested her weight on the rough bark of the railing. It was a lovely spot, it had peace and beauty, and yet she alone of her troubled family seemed able to enjoy it. She sighed again, more heavily, and a line appeared between her brows. The family should learn to enjoy the finer things of life—to be able to absorb beauty such as this, to be calmed and uplifted by it instead of craving the excitement of people and noise.

She thought of them as she had left them tonight, sitting around the chintz and wicker living room, bored because there were no bright lights, no screaming crowds of people. She had asked if any one of them wanted to go for a walk with her and had been more or less courteously, but very definitely, refused.

There was Dick, her husband, who could at least have made an effort and pretended to enjoy a moonlight stroll with her, but he had merely observed that the sound of crickets depressed him, and he intended to stay in the house and stick cotton in his ears. She really didn't care, though. It was surprising how little he mattered to her any more. And yet she had been so thrilled with him when they were married some years ago. He was a splendid-looking creature, tall and well-built and blond, with a golden skin and dark blue eyes. But he had not worn well. They had never been able to talk about anything that interested them both, and she realized now that his layer of glamour was very thin. If you scratched at it, you could see through to a vain, shallow, lazy parasite. He spent her money like water, not on himself, admittedly, but on everyone around him, herself included. He was generous enough, even with the odd bits of money that he made himself. But he had never stayed in any job, and never would, she thought wryly, as long as her money was there to cushion him, unless someone offered him a vice-presidency somewhere that didn't include any real work.

Well, that was Dick, and there wasn't much to be done about it.

Her thoughts drifted to Aunt Sally, who was the only member of her household to claim a blood relationship with her. Sally Frame was in her fifties, but she still gilded her upswept hair, carmined her mouth and nails to match and, without a doubt, looked extremely attractive in her carefully chosen clothes It was through Sally, Gloria remembered, that she had first met Dick Rouston and his sister Rose. Sally and the Roustons were great friends, and she had brought them to the house. At first there was Dick and some of his girlfriends, and then Rose and her husband, Martin Daly. Gloria had been twenty-two, and it was easy enough for Dick Rouston to sweep her off balance.

Dick and Martin had subsequently gone off to the war, and poor Martin had been killed, but of course Dick came gloriously home with not so much as a scratch on him. He had largely, and entirely on his own initiative, offered Rose and her daughter Betsy a home with himself and Gloria, and had been eagerly accepted.

Gloria stirred and eased her weight back from the wooden railing of the narrow little bridge. It was all right about Rose, of course. She was glad enough to give her and Betsy a home, but they spent her money nearly as fast as Dick did. At least they had until she'd been forced to close out all the charge accounts and give them—Sally, Rose, Betsy, and Dick—a daily allowance. It was no use giving them a weekly allowance because they invariably spent the entire sum in two days at the outside. How furious they had all been! And yet she'd had to do it, or there'd have been an end to her money, sooner or later. Betsy, who was a lovely young thing, slim, with reddish brown hair and dark blue eyes like Dick's, had declared that it made her feel as though she were on the dole. Rose, who was usually gay and undeniably good company, had maintained a silence that was full of reproach. She had ostentatiously given up her reducing class, and had taken to measuring her hips with a tape whenever Gloria was there to see it. She had become little heavy with the years but was still pretty and attractive, with her brown, carefully groomed hair, and large blue eyes that were paler in color than those of her daughter and her brother. She had a faithful admirer in Pete Hoge, who followed them each summer to the garish beach resorts that seemed to please them. Color and noise and people—that seemed to be all they wanted. But this year Gloria had insisted upon a quiet retreat in the mountains, and she knew that they were all angry and resentful about it, even Pete Hoge, who, although he was not actually a member of her household, ate enough of her meals to keep him fairly sleek.

Gloria frowned into the moonlight and touched the brown braids that were wound tightly around her head. Dick had never liked her braids, and she could remember her early disappointment when she had unraveled them, expecting admiration, and he had tried to persuade her to change to a long bob that would frame her face. He had declared that the braids accentuated her nose, which was long and beaky with a slight hook. She'd fallen off a horse years ago and broken it, and it had not been set very well. Dick had always insisted that an operation would restore its beauty and change her face entirely, but she could never see that it mattered very much.

She had always been a little bewildered by her sense of isolation from the other members of her household. They could laugh and chatter together by the hour, including faithful and ever-present Pete Hoge, but if she joined in, it was as though a teacher had suddenly entered a classroom of children. They called her The Brain, because she had done rather well at college, and although they were polite enough, they never had much to say to her. If she tried to join in the talk and laughter, it always fell flat, and their courtesy somehow made it all the more pointed. The fact was that they did not like her, and she might as well face it, and that included Dick. And she was sick and tired of the whole thing. A tear dripped from the corner of her eye, and she brushed it away angrily. Self-pity was no good. It was entertaining and comforting while you indulged in it, but it was a destructive emotion and got you nowhere. She gave her head a quick little shake and drew a long breath. She could not be like the rest of them. She was an oddity. Might as well forget it.

She began to hum softly and so did not hear the cautious step directly behind her. She gasped and then screamed shrilly as someone grasped at her legs, tipped her over the frail wooden railing, and sent her hurtling into space.

CHAPTER 2

SHE SEEMED to be smothering in a mass of leaves and twigs, and she moved fretfully. An ominous cracking sound under her back cleared her head a little and warned her to be still. Her body had caught in the branches of a tree, and she realized confusedly that it had saved her life but that she must be infinitely cautious if she were not still to go crashing down onto the rocks below. She moaned and then cut the sound off sharply with a swift intake of breath. Someone had been up there on the bridge, and might still be waiting to push her again.

Her confusion began to drop away, and she realized with a rush of fear and anger that someone had deliberately toppled her over the railing of the bridge and only the chance of an overhanging tree had saved her from instant death.

She stretched a tentative, careful arm, and with a little sob of relief felt her hand close on a fairly substantial bough. She pulled, slowly at first and then with more confidence, and began to edge her weight in toward the trunk. She wore a heavy shoulder pouch bag, and she longed to be rid of it, since its weight and awkwardness hampered her every movement, but it held nearly two thousand dollars, and her accustomed care of it in the last few days held over into her state of confusion and pain.

Afterward, she had not the faintest idea of how long it had taken her to inch her way down that tree to solid ground, nor of how long she lay, face down, dropping bitter tears into the moss that surrounded its base. Physical pain eventually forced her to her feet and brought her thoughts to some sort of order. Her right ankle throbbed angrily, and she could feel blood dripping down the right side of her face. She pulled a handkerchief from her pocket, crushed it against her cheek, and limped painfully out from under the tree. She'd have to get back home somehow, but the terrain was unfamiliar here, and she had no idea which direction to take. She began to push through the under-growth, her mind fixed on the road. Surely she'd come to the road, if she could only keep going long enough. It was queer, she thought vaguely, that the assault had not included robbery as well. It was wrong, of course, to carry so much money around with her, but she'd made up her mind and announced to the others that she'd write no checks during the entire vacation, and she'd given them each a sum that she'd warned them was to last until they got home again. But she'd known that a reserve would be needed. Things were always cropping up, and so she'd brought the extra money. No one had known that she had it, certainly. She always kept her bag with her. It was a habit she had, because she was forever needing it. It held her handkerchief, cigarettes, checks to be written, and cash.

She tripped over a rock and fell, flinging her hands out to protect her injured face. The pain in her ankle was worse, and she was sticky with the blood from her cheek. Fatigue dragged at her like a leaden weight, but she stumbled to her feet and went on, her anxious eyes searching for a light. She had no idea where she was now. She'd never had any sense of direction. The trees, with their pale wash of moonlight, seemed to close in on her ominously.

Why would a tramp, or vagrant, or whoever it was, push her over the bridge without first snatching her bag? It was more than queer. There was some menace in it, only she was too tired just now to figure it out.

Quite suddenly she saw a light, not too close, but gleaming steadily through the trees, and she began to hurry. Her ankle was throbbing with a dull, angry persistence now, and the handkerchief that she still held pressed against her cheek was saturated with blood. But she must push on to that light, she thought grimly. It meant people, and help of some sort. She supposed the family must be looking for her by now, but realized at once that more probably they were in bed and asleep. There was nothing for them to do in a remote, quiet spot like this, so they went to bed early.

She should never have brought them here. She ought to have let them go to one of their noisy, shrill resorts and come here by herself. But of course they wouldn't have liked that, because of the money. It put too much emphasis on the fact that she was supporting them, and they preferred not to think of it in that way. They liked to pretend that they were simply careless about money, and merely used each other's as it became convenient. She had lost count of the times that Dick had touched her for something like a hundred dollars and then sent her a gorgeous bouquet of flowers and a magnificent box of candy just to show how generous he was. The rest of them applauded him warmly and told each other that he was a fine husband.

They were all so gay, and she was so serious, worrying over their extravagances and trying to stop them from spending so much money. It would be better if she didn't have the money, and then she would never have known any of them except Sally, who was a relative and unavoidable. They were not her kind, and there was no common level on which she and they could mix. Only in that case she would have missed the tremendous happiness of having married her first great love, and there was no use in thinking that she'd have been better off without it. It had been a wonderful and thrilling experience, and she wouldn't have missed it for anything. But it was over now, and she ought to finish with it, and with all of them.

Unexpectedly she broke through underbrush and came upon a narrow dirt road. On the other side there was a small house where the light she had been following burned steadily at one of the windows. She gritted her teeth and limped the remaining distance until she found herself at the door. Her head was whirling a little now, but she knocked sharply. She was thinking confusedly, "I must finish with it, and quickly, too. It's almost too late—"

The door opened, and a woman stood before her. Gloria tried to speak, but the woman cried "Merciful heavens!" and pulled her inside. She found herself sitting in a chair and knew that she was going to faint, but she must say something first, something of the utmost importance, something that would keep her hidden from the family so that they would not find her.

"I came up from the city for the day," she said quite clearly. "I've had an accident and missed my train back."

She closed her eyes and dropped her head against the back of the chair. She could faint now. No one would find her for a day or two, and then she'd be stronger.

Which one of them had done it? They were all lazy, extravagant, apparently amiable, all gay, attractive, popular, and yet one of them had tried to murder her.

CHAPTER 3

THE ROOM WAS a cheerful yellow, with the sun pouring in through bright, clean curtains at the window. Gloria stirred, yawned, and then turned her head carefully on the pillow. The door stood open, and she could smell coffee and bacon, and there was the sound of someone singing. The radio, perhaps. The voice took two high notes, and Gloria closed her eyes for a moment and shook her head. Not the radio. There was a mean level of requirement even for radio singers, and although this voice was delivered with confidence, its timber and training would have been better suited for hog calling.

Gloria raised herself in the bed and gingerly touched the bandage on the right side of her face. Her ankle was strapped up, too, and she remembered that there had been a doctor, Dr. Smith. The woman who had taken her in was Mamie, and there was a nephew named John. John had gone for the doctor. She had tried to tell him to get her own doctor, Dr. Zentron, who had recommended this spot in the mountains to her and who, she knew, was spending a vacation week or two in his own cabin in the vicinity, but she had been too exhausted to make her wishes clear.

Mamie's shrill, cheerful song came closer and then trailed off as her head appeared around the door.

"Ah, you're awake, my dear." She seemed delighted about it. "It's nice to see you in your right mind again."

Gloria laughed. "It was awfully good of you to take me in last night. I'm very grateful."

"Oh, nonsense," said Mamie. "How are you feeling, anyway? Ready for some breakfast?"

"Smells delicious." Gloria smiled. "I'll see how my ankle is behaving." She threw the covers back, and then hastily pulled them up again when it was revealed that the yellow lace-bedecked nightgown she was wearing ended abruptly at her waist.

Mamie let out a shriek of laughter. "I'll get you something to put over that. It's an old nightie I had, and I cut the bottom off because I needed it for a skirt. It was just the right color, and I inserted a band of red at each side. It came out fine. But look, you're not supposed to get up. Dr. Smith said you were to stay in bed for two or three days."

"Oh no," Gloria said, her face pinching a little. "I have to—I mean I can't impose on you any longer. I must—"

"Impose, my foot," Mamie hooted, and anchored a straying lock of dry varicolored hair firmly on top of her head. "Listen, Jane," she added, and went on to explain, "We call you Jane because you wouldn't tell us your name last night. What is it, by the way?"

Jane. Plain Jane. Well, there could be no doubt that it was more suitable than Gloria. Her parents had died too early to explain their choice of such a name for her, but she had always wondered what possessed them. She sent Mamie a slow smile, and said, "You must be psychic. My name *is* Jane."

"Well, I never!" Mamie's voice was full of wonder at her own powers. "You know, I've often thought I had second sight. The minute I laid eyes on you, I said, 'There's Jane, for a fact.' "

Gloria tried to spread amazement and admiration over her face and knew she had not succeeded when Mamie asked anxiously, "What's the matter, dear? Do you have a pain somewhere?"

Gloria pulled the light spread from the top of the bed and draped it around her as she got carefully to her feet.

"I'm all right. I feel very well."

She took a few tentative steps and found that the ankle was not impossible, although she had to walk with a great deal of care. Mamie hovered about her, protesting this flouting of the doctor's orders and admiring the courage that produced it all in one breath.

They went out to the kitchen, and Gloria dropped into a chair with a little breath of relief. She was glad she had made the effort, for she had always disliked breakfast in bed and was firmly determined not to impose on Mamie's kindness.

The breakfast was delicious, and when they had finished she dried dishes and listened to Mamie's life history, which was quite interesting.

Afterward, still wrapped in the bedspread, she sat on the front porch in the sun while Mamie did what she called her chores. It was a bad hour for Gloria, for she faced her situation directly, in a manner that was characteristic of her. Someone had attempted to murder her, and there was no use in hiding from the fact. Nor could she believe that it had been a stranger, since there was no attempt at robbery. One of her own household, then, one of her own, had tried to kill her. She should have done some straight thinking sooner, for even before this dreadful climax, her way of living had dropped to a low ebb.

Things would have to be changed. They could not go on in the same way. But first, before anything else, she must learn which one of them had done this awful thing. But how could she find out? And afterward, how could she get rid of them all and start again? It would mean giving away all her money. They'd go quietly and be glad to go, if they had enough money. But it would take all she had to fix them up. They couldn't live cheaply. They weren't used to it.

She laughed out loud and then wondered a little at herself. It was a rare thing for her to laugh. She really ought to have done more of it. Her family laughed a great deal and had hosts of friends, while she herself had very few friends. She must have grown sour, sour and prim. No wonder one of them had pushed her over the bridge to get rid of her. She was a blight on all of them. Perhaps she should have tried to become like them and enjoyed their company, instead of attempting to force them to go her way. But of course the situation could never be natural and easy as long as they were spending her money. She frowned into the sunshine and then dropped her head against the back of her chair.

John Cowrer, Mamie's nephew, had appeared at the door in dressing gown and slippers and was leaning against the jamb, looking at her. She had not heard him, and he was able to make an appraisal at his leisure. She was, he decided, quite a sight. Long, brown braids, unbrushed and untidy, the right side of her face bandaged, and that crooked nose. The worried look on her face did nothing to help, either. Eyes a deep violet color and her skin smooth and ivory-tinted. Not yellow, definitely ivory. Also, she was young, and he seemed to remember from the night before that she was nicely made. It would have been impossible to tell this morning, with that bed-spread draped around her.

He shifted his weight from the jamb and walked out onto the porch.

"Good morning. Feeling a little better?"

Gloria started and clutched at the spread. "I—I'm very well, thank you."

He sat down beside her. "What do you mean, 'very well'? You're a mess. You've an ankle that I heard the doctor order to bed for three days, and yet I don't suppose Mamie carried you out here. Nor did Smith put that bandage on your face to keep it warm."

"It's nothing," Gloria murmured in some confusion. "I can walk pretty well, and I'll get the doctor to take the bandage off my face today. It isn't bleeding now. Then, if I can get a shampoo and a bath, I'll be all right."

Only, she wasn't all right. How could she be, when one of her own family had thrown her over a bridge to get rid of her?

"I'll send a telegram to your people, if you'll give me a name and address," John said, looking at her with a faint curiosity in his dark eyes.

"Telegram?" she echoed stupidly.

"Yes, of course. You were expected back in the city last night, were you not?"

"Oh. Oh no, I—I live alone, and no one expected to see me today. I can go back tonight. I have to get back to work tomorrow."

Tomorrow was Monday, so that sounded reasonable, she thought. And yet, why was she going on with this foolish deception? Why didn't she simply get up and go home now? She'd have to face them all sometime. And she was creating an embarrassing situation, for she had learned during Mamie's autobiography that John was opening a law office in Gloria's own home town. She'd be bound to see him there. What would he think of all these silly lies? He looked like a good, solid individual, tall and rugged. Why hadn't she married someone like him instead of that elegant nuisance, Dick Rouston?

"I don't know whether Smith will take that bandage off today," John was saying. "He seemed to think you were lucky. Said you'd certainly have a scar, but that it was right in the middle of your cheek, and would look exactly like a dimple. It ought to be pretty. Your friends won't know you."

Your friends won't know you. No, she thought suddenly, they wouldn't. And her family wouldn't know her, either. Apparently she had acquired a dimple. But that was just the beginning. There were those jacket crowns you could get on your front teeth that made them look like an advertisement. And then she'd cut her hair off and have it dyed red. The crooked nose would have to be straightened and made shorter by a plastic surgeon, and she'd need some striking new clothes, something quite different from the quiet, conservative things she'd been accustomed to wearing. After that, perhaps a job with this John in her own town, so that she'd have an excuse for being there and also a living. They couldn't get along without a lot of money, but she could.

She was conscious, suddenly, of a fierce, burning anger. She'd find out, if it took the rest of her days, which one of them had tried to kill her.

CHAPTER 4

THE TRAIN clacked along comfortably, and Gloria stared out at the scenery without really seeing anything. She was Jane now, she thought uneasily, and she must forget Gloria entirely so that she would not make a mistake. She must never answer to that name, she must not even think of it in connection with herself, although, as a matter of fact, she looked more like a Gloria now than she ever had before. There was still a little sense of shock every time she looked into a mirror.

Her nose was short and straight, with perfect lines, and her teeth were white and even. It had hurt, having the teeth done, but it was worth it. And then the dimple, just as the doctor had said. It looked, not like a scar, but like any ordinary dimple. She was so completely changed that there hadn't actually been any need to have her hair dyed, but she'd done it anyway. It hung softly about her face in a long bob, its color a vivid golden red.

John had objected to a few things: the red hair, the long red fingernails, and the delicate makeup on her face, which took some time to apply properly. But she'd insisted, because she could not take any chance of being recognized. He'd objected most strongly of all to the sort of clothes she'd wanted, and in fact she'd had to be content with a quieter type of dressing, since he'd refused to allow her to get anything else, and he'd been paying for it. It had all cost so much—the operation on her nose, the dental work, and the expert dyeing of her hair. She hadn't enough for it herself, although she had sold her engagement and wedding rings. There was nothing left for her trousseau, and John had had to buy it.

She glanced sideways at him, sitting there beside her, so big and solid and dependable, his eyes on his newspaper. For a moment a familiar fear rose in her, and she turned her head quickly toward the window again. She had always been so rigidly honest, just, and law-abiding. The family had laughed at her about it, and now she had committed bigamy. She had married John while she was still married to Dick. Well, nobody knew it but herself, and at least she was thoroughly capable of keeping a secret. Perhaps that would make it easier for her to find out which one of them had tried to kill her, for she intended to find out if it took the rest of her life.

It was lucky that John had fallen in love with her. It was much better for her purpose to be his wife than simply a worker in his office. It would give her a great deal more time, and her social contacts would be infinitely better. She needed social contacts, so that she would be invited into the house—her house. It was not a large town, and she would be sure to meet them all sooner or later. It frightened her a little, but she never once thought of abandoning any part of her plan. She'd need plenty of assurance, and she must just look them straight in the eye. They wouldn't know her. How could they? And they would not be able to use up her money for seven years. Must a person have disappeared for seven years, she wondered, before he could be presumed dead? Something like that. Perhaps she could ask John. He was a lawyer, and he'd be sure to know. On the other hand, it would be safer not to ask him a question like that, no matter how casually. He had no lack of intelligence, and he was already a little too interested in the fact that she had no relatives or friends. She had written to a mythical aunt, and he had asked her three times why she had received no reply. She'd have to answer that letter sometime soon.

The train slowed to a stop, and John leaned across and peered out of the window. "Ours is the next stop," he said, with his mind still on his paper.

Jane nearly said "no," but bit it back in time, and John corrected himself. "Next but one, that is."

She smiled at him. "I wish you'd tell me something about our house."

A slightly bothered line appeared between his eyebrows, and he said slowly, "It isn't what I'd have chosen for you, but there was very little to be had and we must live somewhere."

Jane nodded amiably. As a matter of fact, she was not particularly interested. As he said, they had to live somewhere.

"You'll have fun furnishing the place," John said presently. "There's enough there now to get along with, and I arranged to have it thoroughly cleaned."

Jane nodded again abstractedly. It seemed so absurd to go out and buy furniture when she had too much already. She could have taken enough from her own home, without there being any appreciable difference, to have furnished John's entire house.

She laughed a little, and John glanced at her. "What is it?"

"Nothing much." She laughed again. "My aunt always maintained that I had no taste in interior decoration. You should see her house. There's so much stuff that you have to be careful not to trip over it."

"We must pay her a visit as soon as we're settled," he suggested, with the faintest hint of question in his voice.

"Yes. Of course." She turned her eyes away to the window, and thought nervously that she'd have to arrange a quarrel between herself and the nonexistent aunt.

They were nearing the station now, and she was conscious of an uncomfortable fluttering in her stomach. She must be careful not to recognize anybody or anything. She must look everybody straight in the eye and try to keep her face friendly and a bit vague.

The train slowed to a stop, and John got up. She followed him with her nervousness sharpening into actual terror. It was a very small town. She knew everybody and everyone would know her. She must have been mad to think she could get away with such a thing. She stumbled down the steps onto the platform and was conscious of several people standing around, but she dared not raise her eyes to look at any one of them. It was no use. Everyone was bound to know her, and she would go to jail for having two husbands.

"What's the matter?" John asked and added with kindly impatience, "Come on, we must find a taxi of some sort." She tried to smile at him. At the same time she sent a quick, terrified glance around her and saw to her astonishment that no one was even looking at her. It restored her shattered confidence, and she drew a deep breath and hurried after John. She saw that he was making for Sam Brinkerhoff, who had been driving a battered old hack around town ever since she could remember. She started to protest that Sam was a menace on any road, and would probably land them and their luggage in a ditch, and had to swallow it when she realized that Sam was supposed to be a stranger to her.

John turned to her and helped her into the sagging old car with a hand on her arm. Sam touched his cap and called her "miss," and she relaxed with a relieved little sigh, since it had always been "ma'am" in the days of Gloria.

They started off and Sam asked chattily, "Strangers, ain'tcha?"

"No," said John. "We were born and brought up here."

Sam turned and gave them a long stare, leaving the car to steer itself. "Never seen you before in my life," he observed, and bumped the rear wheel over a curb as he turned a corner.

"Don't go so fast," John said sharply, and Sam speeded up a little, while Jane leaned back, closed her eyes, and waited for the crash.

However, nothing happened, and she presently opened her eyes and realized at once that they were heading in the general direction of her own home. She wondered uneasily what he could have bought out this way. She could think of nothing that had been for sale.

"Here we are," John said cheerfully. "Wake up, Jane, this is the place."

She couldn't believe it. It was impossible. Just an old house, so old that it had a reputation for being haunted—and it was her own property! How could they have sold it, when it belonged to her?

It meant that she had not merely disappeared. She was dead.

CHAPTER 5

JANE LONGED to ask how the crumbling old house could possibly have been made livable. She got slowly out of the car and stood looking at the bay windows and the ornate wooden fretwork that draped the porch.

"It hasn't been painted on the outside yet," John said, a little anxiously. "They'll be starting on that next week. It was included in the price."

"How much did you pay for it?" she asked, her eyes moving up to the cupola at the top.

John told her, and she drew in her breath sharply. How could they have charged such a price! It was nothing less than dishonest. And how could John, who was so careful of his money, have paid it?

Anger held her silent, and John thought she was disappointed. He gave her arm a little squeeze and urged her forward.

"Suppose we go inside. It's been cleaned up and redecorated. I know it doesn't look like much on the outside, but it'll be better when it's painted."

She moved on obediently, but he knew that she was unconscious of the affectionate pressure of his hand on her arm. He wondered why he had so much feeling for this odd, contradictory girl. He realized that she had not much feeling for him, although she did not dislike him. But she seemed to move in a mist of her own abstraction, and he often wondered what she was thinking about during her long silences.

They went into the house, and Jane gave a little gasp.

"You see?" John said eagerly. "It's nice, isn't it? Clean and fresh. It's a little fancy, perhaps, but I expect it's all right. I know very little about interior decorating."

Fancy. Yes, and right up to and beyond the current style. Jane recognized immediately the handiwork of Sally and Rose. She could well imagine the fun they'd had fixing up this old wreck.

As John escorted her over the house, she had some difficulty in restraining her laughter. In most of the rooms there were two different wallpapers, one wall always more violent than the other three. Well, it must be the latest style, or they wouldn't have done it. The bedrooms could be neatly labeled the Pink Room, the Blue Room, the Yellow Room. When they came to the Green Room, Jane looked it over and said, "Phooey!"

"You don't like it?" John asked.

She laughed out suddenly. "On the contrary, I do like it. I like it very much. But isn't it going to be expensive to get matching furniture for all this elaborate inside scenery?"

"We can take it slowly. We have a thousand dollars, a couple of beds, two chairs, and a dining-room table, and when we add our wedding presents we can make out for a while."

Jane nodded and felt color burning in her face. All the wedding presents had come from his side. She ought to have sent some things to herself with different name cards attached. Only she had no money, nothing except what John gave her. It was odd to be on the receiving end. But she knew John's position of dispenser only too well, and she found it impossible to ask for anything more than was absolutely necessary.

John said a little heavily, "Well, how is it, Jane? Do you like it, or does it seem depressing to you?"

She roused herself and said quickly, "It's lovely, John. I like it all immensely. It's going to be tremendously interesting to get it all furnished and fixed up. And then, when it's painted on the outside, it will be simply perfect."

He brightened up immediately and said, "I have a real surprise for you, something that seems to be very rare these days."

He led her downstairs and out to the kitchen, and the surprise was more of a shock to her than he could have guessed.

It was Dolly. She had employed Dolly from time to time during the past years, and they looked at each other for a moment of silence which seemed to Jane to stretch out endlessly. She could not speak, she did not even breathe, and she was conscious of a singing in her ears.

Dolly's face relaxed into a familiar, wide grin, and she said amiably, "Glad to know you, ma'am, I'm sure."

Jane drew a long, quivering breath and smiled back. It strengthened her confidence enormously to realize that this woman, who had been familiar to her since she was a little girl, was greeting her as an absolute stranger.

There was a prolonged ring of the front doorbell, and Dolly, as was usual with her, flew off to get there first and find out who it was.

"She's a full-time maid," John said proudly. "She offered herself at a very reasonable figure, so I took her on. She may turn out to be impossible, of course, but in that case you can always get rid of her."

"Oh, I hope I shan't have to do that."

It was exactly like Dolly, she thought, to offer herself at a low wage so that she could get inside the house and satisfy her curiosity about the new couple. She more or less lived on gossip, and she might turn out to be very helpful in supplying information about the other house. She'd have to keep Dolly. And she knew how to do it too. Simply feed her an unending stream of confidential anecdotes.

Dolly returned at that moment and, unexpectedly, they heard Mamie's cheerful voice behind her. They had not seen Mamie since she had come down to New York to manage their wedding for them. She was usually at loose ends in the winter, since her house in the mountains was apt to be isolated with the first snowstorm, and so far this winter had proved very entertaining. She had arrived now to help the newlyweds put their house in order. She explained this several times, very volubly, as she knew perfectly well that she should not have come, but she had not been able to resist. When it appeared that they did not seem to mind, she was vastly and noisily relieved.

As a matter of fact, Jane was glad. She knew that with Mamie and Dolly both on the scene, she would be entirely relieved of household cares, and she had other things to do.

John said kindly, "Glad to see you, Mamie. I'm sure you'll be a help to Jane. But we'll have to get into town and buy another bed today. We were going to buy one tomorrow or the next day, anyway."

Mamie protested to high heaven. She didn't need a bed . She

could sleep anywhere, perhaps on the couch in the living room. What was wrong with the living-room couch?

John grinned at her. He knew that she had several friends who had named their living-room couches after her. She had to go somewhere during the winter, and she could not afford much, so she made the rounds of her friends and then returned their hospitality at her house in the mountains when summer came.

"I'm glad you're here, Mamie," Jane said pleasantly. "You can help me choose the furniture. We'll go and get the bed today, because we have no living-room couch as yet."

Mamie was delighted. There was nothing she liked better than choosing furniture, and she insisted on seeing the room in which the bed was to go before they bought it.

They took her through the entire house, and she cheerfully and verbally tore the decorating to pieces. She was particularly scornful at the idea of having one wall in a room different from the other three.

"What will the idiots think of next?" she demanded. "You might as well cut an oriental rug in half and put that down, and have kitchen linoleum on the other half of your floor."

John laughed, but Jane, standing at the window, had frozen into a terrified silence.

Dick Rouston was coming in at the gate.

CHAPTER 6

JANE NEVER TOOK her eyes off Dick Rouston as he walked slowly and with his usual careless grace up the path toward the front door. He mounted the steps to the porch and disappeared from her view, but still she stood there, her heart thudding violently, her mind racing over and over again, foolishly, to the single phrase, "There goes my legal husband."

She waited rigidly for the bell to ring, but Mamie had time to say curiously, "What are you looking at out there, Jane?" before it pealed through the house.

John left the room, and Jane turned to Mamie with a smile that was stretched like a gash across her face. She must talk, make light conversation, and smile a lot. The new teeth would distract attention from her mouth. But the mouth was different. It must be different, with all the lipstick on it. And, after all, Dolly hadn't known her.

"What on earth's the matter?" Mamie asked. "You look as though you might be going to faint."

Jane swallowed twice and began to talk very rapidly.

"I was wondering, Mamie, what sort of furniture we ought to get for the living room. Modernistic, maybe—only that wouldn't suit this old house, would it? Chippendale, perhaps, or Sheraton, or early American. Oh no—Victorian. That would be exactly right."

They were coming up the stairs now. She could hear John's voice and Dick's conversing amiably together.

Mamie said, "Omigod! Victorian! Terrible!"

"Oh no, you're wrong," Jane said feverishly, twisting her hands together. "It isn't supposed to be terrible any more. It's being done a lot."

"You going to get a piano?"

"Yes, of course. Yes, certainly. A piano."

John's voice said "Jane," and she knew that they were in the room, but she could not turn her head. She wondered, in her panic, why Dick was so much harder to meet than Dolly had been. She hadn't minded Dolly half so much. But Dolly was stupid, of course, and Dick was shrewd and quick. Much too quick.

She forced herself to turn around and stood stiff and motionless as John introduced them. She put on a bright smile, murmured something conventional, and then wished wildly that she had tried to change her voice. Had he seemed a little startled when she spoke? Or was it just her imagination? She must pull herself together.

"I wanted to be sure that the furnace was working properly, Mrs. Cowrer," Dick said easily. "I didn't want you people to be shivering here. I know the firm that installed it, and I'd be able to get quicker action if there were anything wrong."

"Is it a new furnace?" Jane asked, feeling like a stupid child.

Dick gave her a charming smile, "Oh yes, brand new. The old one more or less fell apart when they touched it and had to be carried out in small pieces." He smiled again, and his dark blue eyes swept their faces. "We've had a good many headaches over the rehabilitation of this place, as a matter of fact. Trouble with the workmen, difficulty in getting materials. Actually, it was started last September and now, in March, they still haven't painted the outside. But I think that's arranged at last, and they should be starting on it very soon."

They had started work on the house in September, and she was supposed to have died at the beginning of August. But how could they have laid their greedy hands on her estate so quickly?

Dick dismissed the troubles caused by the house with a faint shrug and offered her a cigarette in the familiar slim silver case. She took one and then wished that she had refused. It was such an accustomed gesture—Dick offering a cigarette, and Gloria taking it and holding it to his light.

"Who did the inside decorations here, Mr. Rouston?" Mamie asked.

Dick glanced at her, and Jane could see the quick appraisal that he made. She knew that Mamie was instantly relegated to the hordes of the unimportant, although he answered with perfect courtesy, "My aunt and my sister. They're very fond of this sort of thing. But I must not forget that they sent me over here to invite you to dinner. They knew that you'd be busy getting settled in, and they felt that it would relieve the pressure if you didn't have to bother about dinner."

"That's extremely good of you," John said heartily, "but my aunt is with us, and we had planned to have something in town."

Dick turned to Mamie with a little bow, and said that of course she must come, too, and Mamie, quite unaware that he had placed her as an utter outsider, fell an instant victim to his charm.

"Why not?" she appealed to John. "It will make the shopping simpler. All we have to bother about is something for breakfast, and the bed, of course." She added a little anxiously, "You were going to buy the bed anyway, weren't you, John?"

"Yes, of course," he assured her.

"Because if you weren't, I could always put up at the hotel."

"Don't be silly, Mamie," Jane said hastily. "We had definite plans for buying that bed. I have an aunt, too, you know, and we'll need it for her as well. But I don't think we should impose ourselves on Mr. Rouston's family for dinner. We can easily get a meal in town when we've finished with the shopping."

Dick sent her one of his quick glances and took a step in her direction. "Please come, Mrs. Cowrer, or I shall be in trouble at home. The ladies of my household sent me over here with most explicit instructions. You see, your aunt and your husband are agreeable." He gestured vaguely toward the other two. "We shall expect you at seven." He smiled around at all of them, backed to the door, and was gone.

Now he'll go home and break the news to Sally and Rose that there will be guests for dinner, Jane thought. They wouldn't care, though. Probably there would be other guests. Perhaps some of the regular gang with whom they used to go around. She'd have to meet them all at once, and she was frightened. And why had Dick persisted with the invitation? Certainly it was not concern for the comfort of three strangers. There must have been another reason.

"Very nice neighbors," John said. "Very kind of them. Well, I think we'd better be getting into town and see about that bed."

Dolly's head appeared around the door, and she asked in a stage whisper, "Is he gone?"

"Are you referring to the gentleman who just left?" Mamie asked coldly.

"Yeah, him. I didn't want to bump into him, because he's good and mad at me. I been workin' for him and he offers me a hatful of money to stay." She gave a reminiscent little sigh over the hatful of money and went on. "But me, I like to live where I'm happy. Over there, they got an old woman does the cooking and her and me don't hit it off, and they always stick up for her. That ain't right, and I told them so. Now, when Mrs. Dick was living, she'd be fair. Always listened and tried to fix things up. But the rest of that bunch, when I tell them what goes on, they just say, 'Oh, shut up,' or something."

"Mr. Rouston is a widower?" John asked, while Mamie looked interested in spite of herself.

"Yeah, sure, but you don't have to hang up no crepe for him. He don't care. He's got the money, and he ain't tied down no more. Poor Miss Gloria. I don't know but what sometimes I think she done it on purpose."

Mamie, now only faintly aware that she should not be listening to the gossip of a servant, asked eagerly, "What did she do? What happened to her?"

"Drownded," Dolly supplied mournfully. "In a river. She went for a walk near a waterfall, and maybe she slipped and maybe the poor soul jumped. Me, I ain't sayin'. Anyways, they didn't find her body for a week, and when they did—well, they couldn't hardly reckernize her."

CHAPTER 7

JANE SHUDDERED. She had seen a paragraph or two in the newspaper which mentioned her disappearance and added that the river was being dragged for her body, but she had seen nothing about a body having been found. Some other poor creature who had been missing was still missing, then, because she had not come forward, and her family was perhaps still suffering over the uncertainty.

Mamie asked avidly, "How could they tell it was Mrs. Rouston, if she was in such bad shape?"

"Well, it must of been her," Dolly said sensibly. "Her clothes, what was left of them, was sort of nothing much. Nobody couldn't say if they was hers or not. The hair was the same, and anyways, there wasn't no one else missing, so it must of been her."

"The family identified her?" Jane asked, feeling sick. "They were satisfied?"

Dolly nodded vigorously. "Sure. They said it didn't look much like her, but I guess it didn't look like much of anything human. They couldn't remember what dress she had on, and her shoes and pocketbook was missing, and none of that bunch knew anything about her underclothes." Dolly lowered her voice and moved closer to them. "Seems they never seen her in her underclothes, not even her husband. He says to the cops that she never would get undressed in front of him, and he couldn't identify any of her clothes, positively not."

John laughed and said, "Miss Prim, evidently."

Miss Prim. Yes, she had been. There were plenty of rooms in that big house to be prim in. But she hadn't been able to be prim with John. There hadn't been space enough, and somehow she hadn't cared much. She had been consumed by a burning anger, and John was just a means to an end.

John had an arm across her shoulders, and he stooped and kissed her gently on the forehead. "Wake up, darling. We have to buy beds for Mamie and Dolly, not to mention a few other things."

They went downstairs and out to the ancient barn that housed John's new car. Mamie was ecstatic over the car and exclaimed with a satisfied little sigh, "You have everything necessary for a young couple to start out with. You're lucky, even if you do have wallpaper that doesn't match. But what in the world were those women thinking of to have one wall papered differently from the other three in every room? You know what I think? I bet the paperhangers made a mistake, so those women had them go on doing it to make it look right."

"Oh no," Jane said, rather abruptly. "It's done a lot. Considered quite the thing."

Mamie subsided, looking somewhat abashed, and Jane thought uneasily that, she'd have to get out of that cold, stilted way of speaking. It was too typical of Gloria.

She laughed and looked over her shoulder at the back seat of the car where Mamie now sat in silence. She said gaily that probably that had started the vogue for different wallpapers in the same room, some paperhanger making a mistake. Mamie cheered up at once and went on to suggest a cocktail when they got to town. Jane had never cared for cocktails, but going into bars would enable her to meet the town in a different manner.

John said a cocktail sounded fine, but he thought they should stop at one each. He didn't want Mamie disgracing them with their new neighbors.

Mamie snorted. "So now I'm going to disgrace you. Do you remember the time I took you to the zoo when you were a kid, and—"

"Never mind," John said austerely. "Don't forget that minister relative of yours who had twelve children he couldn't afford, so that his wife had to take in washing secretly."

They went into the hotel and to the cocktail lounge. Jane looked at the gleaming chromium and red leather and remembered how Dick had brought her here, often at first, and then not at all. She was relieved to find that the bartender was a stranger to her.

They sat at a small table and as Mamie drew off her gloves she said thoughtfully, "But he used to help her with the washing after he'd finished his sermon."

"Don't quibble," John said. "What will you have?"

Jane found herself looking squarely into a mirror, and she could not take her eyes off her mirrored face. It was a beautiful face now, young and appealing, with a certain distinction which was left over from Gloria. It was amazing, and it showed what people could do with themselves if they tried. She had always considered herself plain but with a compensating amount of true worth, and as this thought entered her head she saw the face in the mirror assume a slight sneer. John had solid worth. It was his entire makeup, and yet he had paid no attention to her until she'd changed herself, and then he moved in with firm purpose. But, illogically, he was always trying now to change her back to what she had been. Well, at least he could never bring back the old teeth and nose.

"Couldn't you, just for a minute," John said mildly, "stop looking at yourself and give us a little polite conversation?"

Jane dropped guilty eyes from the mirror and laughed in some confusion. "There's something insidious about a mirror in front of you," she murmured.

Mamie, moving her fingers restlessly on the stem of her glass, said, "John, do you think you can stand a small town like this?"

Jane was amused, after her first reaction, to find herself resentful of this implied criticism of her home town.

"Why, I think it's a charming little place," she said defensively.

John nodded. "I'm glad you like it, Jane. You see, I want to go into politics, and it seems to point in this direction. As for Mamie, she lives in a much smaller town than this."

"Only during the summer," Mamie said spiritedly. "In the winter I always live in a big city. This is going to be a change for both of you, and I don't know whether you're going to like it or not."

Jane drank three cocktails, which was one above her usual limit, and then John refused to let her have any more. Mamie continued to imbibe, and John shook his head at her.

"I'm only a young man trying to get along, and liquor's expensive."

"Oh, nuts!" Mamie said loudly. "Don't hand me that line. You've had dusty stacks of money in the bank since away back. You can pay for a few drinks."

"Yes, of course. I saved all my life so that I could afford to buy you cocktails."

"That's better," Mamie said with a satisfied nod. "Now let's go and get that bed, when I finish this next one, that is."

John herded them out after a while and steered them toward the furniture shop. Everyone seemed to be staring at the three of them, and he was aware of feeling a little self-conscious. He wanted to be a leading citizen of this town, and here was his wife, undoubtedly beautiful, but possibly a little too much so. He glanced at the glory of her red-gold hair, curling softly on her shoulders. She wore a blue suit with a matching coat. He remembered that she'd wanted Kelly green, but he had insisted on the blue. The outfit was very plain, no trimming, not even buttons except where they were strictly necessary, and yet it was immensely smart. And she wore no hat. She glowed like a jewel in that country town, and it made him a little uneasy.

He glanced over at Mamie and immediately averted his eyes. Mamie had an unfailing instinct for clothes. She always managed to get the worst combination of color and line that it was possible to obtain.

The two of them had stopped at a shop window and were animatedly discussing the display. John, standing behind them and waiting for them to move on, glanced idly down the street where a blind man was approaching, moving slowly and tapping cautiously in front of him with a cane. John scarcely noticed him, for his mind was on Jane. She was speaking more loudly and volubly than was usual with her. He supposed it was the cocktails. But he liked her voice when she really opened up, it had a warm, lovely quality.

The blind man was abreast of them now, and suddenly he stopped, his cane pointed outward. John looked at him curiously and saw that his lips were trembling.

"Miss Gloria," he said softly. "Miss Gloria."

CHAPTER 8

MAMIE AND Jane went into the shop, and John followed them after casting a vague look at the blind man, whom he presently forgot entirely. They bought a lamp, and John carried it out under his arm and deposited it in the car. The other two went on to the furniture shop, and when John caught up with them he found Mamie standing apart with her brow furrowed, while Jane completed a deal with the salesman.

"She's buying that bed over there," Mamie said in an injured voice. "I wanted her to get this one. It's not only much prettier, but it's cheaper as well."

John looked at it, and raised his eyebrows. "My dear Mamie, we can't furnish that old house in modified Gothic."

"Modified what?" Mamie asked, mystified. "I don't know what you're talking about. This is Early American with a cute touch."

"All right. But we still can't furnish the house with cute touches."

Jane came back looking tired and a little pale. She felt dizzy and was developing a headache, which she attributed to the three cocktails.

"We have to cart the stuff home ourselves," she said tiredly. "Can we do that?"

John nodded. "Mattresses and springs go on the roof, and the rest tied on around the sides." He walked off and went into a huddle with the salesman.

By the time they had returned home and unloaded the bed, Jane's headache was pounding savagely against her temples. She felt entirely too unwell, she thought, to go to the dinner that was to be graciously served her out of her own money and in her own house. She was glad to have an honest excuse for not going, since she was inclined to think she'd have pleaded a headache in any case.

She sent John and Mamie off to keep the engagement, and Dolly was amiable about bringing her a tray in bed. When the tray had been carefully placed on her lap, Dolly said that if it were all right she'd like to run out for a few minutes to look in on her sick uncle. Jane told her to go ahead, knowing full well that she was headed for a local tavern, which she had frequented for years.

After Dolly had gone, Jane ate her supper and then settled back against her pillows with a cigarette. Her head was better, but she was possessed by a restless excitement that would not let her read or sleep. She realized that the white heat of her anger was burning itself out, and in the reaction she felt a little ridiculous. Why was she so resentful, after all, because other people were living on her money and in her house? She had not earned the money herself. It had been left to her, so why not let them have it? She was settled now, nobody knew her, and certainly John was more companionable than Dick had ever been. She could talk to John and be interested in talking with him, while her conversation with Dick had dropped down to a few brief words when they were necessary.

But there was a murderer over there in her house, and you couldn't sit back and let a murderer run around loose. Although there must be many murderers and potential murderers running around loose, so why bother? Only there was a gnawing feeling inside her that would not let her rest. It was so hard for her to live dishonestly.

She wondered what it was that had mitigated her anger. She had realized it only today on her arrival in this house. But she'd have to unearth the truth. There would be no rest for her until she did. That was why she had come here and why she had sacrificed John. She suddenly covered her face with her hands and felt hot tears burning against her eyes. How could she have done such a thing? She who was so honest.

She stretched an arm to the bedside table for her handkerchief and held it against her eyes for a moment. The silence around her was absolute, and she realized that she was alone in this old, old house that was supposed to have been haunted for many years. It had not been occupied for as far back as she could remember, and there was a story connected with it, some silly thing. A girl, crossed in love, who went around playing the piano mournfully all the time, that was it. There were any number of people who were willing to swear that they had heard the piano playing in the empty house, but there hadn't been a piano or any other furniture in the place for as far back as she could remember, before John took over. She had intended for at least a year or two to have the house pulled down, and now look at it. Wallpaper out like a rash in all the rooms, and not the kind she would have chosen herself. Sally and Rose should be living here and enjoying their handiwork.

She wondered suddenly what they had done to her own house. Was there new, sickly wallpaper growing like a fungus over there, too? They had wanted to have the place redecorated some time ago, and she had refused, because she had a great fondness for all the old things that had always been there: the red brocade in the dining room, the faded green silk in the drawing room, and the mellow old wood paneling in the library. The thought that these might all be gone brought her out of bed with a sudden burning anger. She should never have done this insane thing. She should have gone back and not given up what was rightfully hers.

She put on a pale green woolen robe and went to the window, where she stared down into the dark garden.

It was no use regretting anything, she thought. She could never have gone back, anyway. They would have thought her story quite crazy and said so, and there would have been no peace for her, living with them. There would inevitably have been another attempt upon her life.

She was suddenly afraid of that large, old silent house, and she realized that she had been half listening for the sound of a piano. She turned away from the window with a quickly indrawn breath and straightened her back. She'd have to stop that sort of nonsense. It was absurd.

She forced herself to go to the door, out into the hall, and down the echoing stairs. She went along to the kitchen where she turned on the light, and in its cheerful glow she was able to throw off most of her fear. She made fresh coffee and sat down at the table with it.

Dick, she thought, was the one to benefit most by her death, but that didn't prove that he'd pushed her over the bridge. Rose benefited almost as much, since Dick was so fond of her and so easy with his money, and, of course, that applied to Betsy as well. How old was Betsy now? Sixteen, perhaps. Then there was Sally. She would have an inheritance of her own and could continue to live comfortably with the others. And so there it was. They all benefited, and any one of them might have tried to kill her. It was very probable that even Pete Hoge benefited. He and Rose could get married now. Dick wouldn't mind supporting Pete. She had never refused to support Pete herself, but it had not been suggested to her.

She heard the sound of footsteps on the porch, and then John's voice and Mamie's laugh, and she found herself relaxing with a sigh of relief. It was a creepy old place in which to be alone.

She offered them coffee, but John was tired and went up to bed. Mamie sat down with her, and Jane waited anxiously to hear all that she had to tell.

Mamie had much to say, but she couldn't resist offering the juiciest item first. She stirred sugar vigorously into her coffee, and said, "That Rouston man—Dick's his name—well, his wife—her name was Gloria—anyway, it seems she was definitely insane before she committed suicide. The family were about to make arrangements to have her put away."

CHAPTER 9

FOR A MOMENT Jane was seized by a vertigo that forced her to close her eyes and hang onto the table. They were thoroughly vicious, she thought wildly. All of them. They must have planned a thing like that together. Their implacable determination to be rid of her was terrifying even in retrospect, and she thought, "Oh, God! How hideous it would have been if I had gone back!"

Mamie was looking at her curiously. She said, "My dear, don't you feel well? This is the second time today that you've looked as though you might faint. I do hope you're not going to have a baby already. They're cute, but they work you half to death, and anyway, I don't want to be a great-aunt just yet."

Jane gave her a rather crooked little smile. "N—no baby. I'm just tired. But go on, Mamie. Tell me all about them."

Mamie poured more coffee and sugared it, with her lips pursed.

"Well, it seems this wife—this Gloria—was a sort of gloomy creature. Melancholy, they said, and though they were always trying to cheer her up, she got worse and worse. And then last summer they wanted to take her to a resort, one of these gay places where everybody has fun, you know, but she wouldn't go. Insisted on going to the mountains, right near where my place is, as a matter of fact, and when they got there, she took to going off for long walks by herself. Then she'd come back and stalk over and turn the radio off on them."

Well, she had. But she hated a radio blaring from morning till night.

"Then," Mamie said dramatically, "the night she was drowned, she'd gone for one of these long walks, and the family had a conference about her. They all agreed that she needed a doctor's care, and they were going to try and get her to a good man they knew of. But she never came back. They were all out looking for her, for a while, and then they went back home and went to bed. Figuring, you see, that she'd probably turn up, because she was always taking these long walks. But the next morning she was still missing, so they reported it to the police."

John's voice called from upstairs, "Are you two going to sit gossiping there all night, or are you coming to bed?"

They got up from the table, and while Mamie carried the dishes to the sink, Jane watched her abstractedly. She'd have to try to keep Mamie around. She seemed to be invaluable at snooping. Probably it was Sally who had opened up. Sally had never been able to keep anything to herself. Dick and Rose could be quite as voluble, but they didn't give anything away, and Betsy was interested only in her own affairs.

She went up to the bedroom, where John smiled at her and kissed her tenderly. "I'm sorry we couldn't have had dinner in our own place, darling, on our first night here."

"Oh, well." She brushed it aside good-naturedly. "It was a good thing, really. If you're going in for politics, you'll have to go in for the social life a bit too."

"I wouldn't have gone without you, though, except for Mamie. I thought that if I removed that red-and-green plaid suit she's wearing, your headache might improve."

Jane laughed. "It did improve, but I don't think the suit was what brought it on."

"The place is pretty bare," John said, his eyes moving over the room, "but we'll try and get it more livable during the weekend."

Jane made no reply. Her mind was involved again with the horror of what she had just heard from Mamie, and she thought savagely that every member of her former family must somehow be rendered incapable of injuring anyone else as they had sought to injure her.

John watched her for a moment, and then he said abruptly, "Jane, what is the matter with you? You don't answer me half the time, and you seem to be miles away in a world of your own."

The sharpness in his voice brought her to attention, and she said hastily, "I'm sorry. I didn't hear you."

"What's on your mind?"

"Why, I—it's the house, John. Ideas for furnishing it and all that. It's so big, you know, that it takes a lot of thinking over."

He said no more, but he did not believe her. She had seemed far away from him ever since they'd boarded the train to come to this place, and he was convinced that something lay heavy on her mind. She had always been rather inarticulate, of course. He really knew nothing whatever about her. But it didn't matter. If she had secrets, she was entitled to keep them, but they must not reach over and shadow her life with him. If something was bothering her, he'd have to clear it up for her, no matter what it was.

He fell into an uneasy sleep at last, but Jane was restless all night. She dozed occasionally and always went into a nightmare that brought her to sweating, trembling wakefulness again.

Breakfast the next morning was plentiful and delicious, but Dolly was sulky because Mamie had been out in the kitchen, trying to show her what to do. She complained about it every time she was in the dining room.

"I ain't fussy, see, and what I don't know about I got to be told, but anybody tries to tell me how to cook, they might as well tell a cat how to catch a mouse." She put the coffeepot on the table with a magazine under it, cast a baleful look at Mamie, and stalked off to the kitchen. She was back in a moment with bacon and eggs.

"Furthermore," she resumed, "I had a longer training than any cook I know, in a plaid suit or out of one, because Ma died early, and I took over when I was seven. The first pie I cooked for Pa, he threw it at my head, and I threw it right back. After that we got on fine."

She departed again for the kitchen, and Mamie said in a low voice, "That's her trouble, if you ask me. She's still cooking the way she did when she was seven."

"Leave her alone, Mamie," John said firmly. "I don't know which of you is the better cook, but collaboration doesn't seem to be feasible."

Mamie laughed heartily and then, on thinking it over, decided to be offended.

"I'm sure I don't want to interfere, John, but that girl is a country yokel and she needs training. Did you hear her refer to my plaid suit?"

But John's eyes were on Jane. He thought she looked better this morning, but the violet eyes still held no awareness of him. She answered him when he spoke to her, briefly and with a smile, but she seemed far away. He presently went off to his office with an increasing feeling of uneasiness.

Through the dining-room window, Mamie saw him drive off in the car, and she let out a wail.

"Jane! He's taken the car! How are we going to get into town—and with all we have to do too."

"I have to take a driver's test and get my license," Jane explained, "and then I'll drive him in every morning, and we can have the car for the rest of the day."

She had a driver's license, had had one for years, but it was in the name of Gloria Rouston.

"Well, but that doesn't help us today," Mamie said aggrievedly.

"We can walk in, Mamie. It's really not very far."

"How do you know? We've only been once in the car, and you can't judge distance that way."

She had walked it hundreds of times—it was a favorite walk of hers—but she merely said, "I'm going to try it, anyway. Come along, if you feel like it."

There was nothing else for Mamie to do, since Dolly was so uncooperative about the housework. She buttoned a cerise coat over the red-and-green plaid suit, tied a yellow handkerchief over her head, and pulled a pair of purple wool gloves out of her suitcase. She doubted whether the purple quite matched her costume, but wool gloves would be warmer on such a long, cold walk.

They started out briskly, and presently came to the Rouston house, set far back from the road amid a dignified assortment of trees and shrubs. Jane gave it a look of distaste. It was a beautiful old place, but she had been very unhappy there.

Betsy came out of the front door and flashed across the snow-covered lawn to the road ahead of them. Jane slowed their pace a little, and Mamie observed with a sniff, "Nothing on her mind but her face, that one."

Jane watched the tall, slim young figure speculatively. Betsy wore a brief skirt and scarlet sweater and was swinging a pair of ice skates by a strap. She presently cut off the road obliquely and headed for the small lake where they skated in the winter and swam in the summer. Jane glanced at her watch and saw that it was nearly eleven. It seemed a little early for Betsy to be out for exercise, and in any case she usually ran around with her own gang. It was unusual for her to go anywhere alone.

But of course she wasn't alone. As she approached the shack where they changed their skates, Jane saw a man step out and place his hands on the girl's shoulders. There was something intimate in the way he looked down into the vivid young face, and suddenly Jane caught her breath. It was all wrong. It shouldn't be Betsy standing there laughing up so gaily into the eyes above her. It should be her mother, Rose.

The man was Pete Hoge.

CHAPTER 10

MAMIE NUDGED Jane's arm and hissed, "Don't stare."

Jane walked on hurriedly and asked into the collar of her coat, "Who is she?"

"That's the niece of the man who owns the place—Dick Rouston, the fellow who invited us to dinner, remember? He certainly is an attractive man, and he doesn't look much older than the girl. The mother doesn't either, for that matter." Mamie took a quick look over her shoulder and added, "That man she's with—he looks like the fellow they called Pete something or other. He must be her boyfriend, although I got the impression last night that he was beauing the mother around—Rose, her name is. There's an aunt—only they don't call her aunt—just Sally. She's young-looking, too, but the wife who died was her niece, and I'll bet she's as old as I am, maybe more. You'd never know it, though, the way she's all fixed up like a young girl."

Jane snuggled her cold chin deeper into her collar. So Pete and Betsy were fooling around. Rose wouldn't like it. Not that she wasn't always going around with other men herself, but it would singe her vanity badly. And Betsy shouldn't be going around with an irresponsible playboy like Pete. Why didn't they look after her better, anyway? Of course Rose would put a stop to it if she knew, and Rose would have to be told. There was no way out of it.

Jane sighed. "We'll drop in and say hello to them on the way back."

"Who?"

"Those people. I must thank them for the dinner invitation and apologize for not showing up."

"O.K.," Mamie agreed amiably. "I'd like to see the house in the daytime anyway, and those women too. Everybody looks better in the night light. But the furniture certainly is fancy. They must have a pile of money."

Jane shivered, and Mamie glanced at her. "Cold?"

"Yes."

"Well, I'm not. I'm all in a glow. I haven't walked so far for years. I knew this was going to be longer than you thought. You just can't judge distance when you're in a car. I wish a car would come this way. I'd thumb a ride for us."

This appalling prospect sent Jane hurrying at a pace that presently brought forth a protest from Mamie.

"For corn's sake, slow up," she panted. "We're not going to a fire."

Jane slowed a little and said almost pleadingly, "It's not far now, Mamie. I'm sure we're almost there. But we can't thumb rides. I couldn't do that."

"Sometimes," Mamie observed, still panting, "you're too proud for your own good. Where's the harm in thumbing a ride? It doesn't hurt anyone, and it would save my feet."

Jane continued to hurry until a turn in the road brought the town rather suddenly before them.

"Well," Mamie said on a long sigh, "the first thing is to find a place where we can get a cup of coffee. My feet need a rest."

Jane knew exactly where to go for a cup of coffee, but she was obliged to trail after Mamie in simulated ignorance while Mamie flitted hither and yon in all the wrong directions. It was some time before Jane was able to maneuver them to the Forget-Me-Not Tea Shop, where she knew that the coffee was excellent.

Mrs. Lucy Singer, proprietor and decayed gentlewoman, still presided at the cash register, Jane noticed, and Gert still waited on the orange-colored tables, with their borders of bright blue forget-me-nots. Gert's jaws worked vigorously on her gum, and she eyed Jane from head to foot with alert interest, but there was no sign of recognition in the look. Lucy merely gave them a glance and returned to her knitting.

They did not know her, obviously, and Jane relaxed over her coffee. She had tried to alter her voice when she spoke to Gert. She usually tried to alter it when she thought of it, but she was always forgetting. It didn't really matter, though. What difference did a voice make?

They spent a busy day. They had a thousand dollars for the furniture, but it was not nearly enough. Mamie could have stretched it a good deal farther, as she kept pointing out, but although Jane remained good-tempered and amiable, she made her own selections and consistently ignored Mamie's advice.

Late in the afternoon they went to the Forget-Me-Not for tea and collapsed wearily onto the orange-colored chairs. Mamie threw back her coat and groaned. "Jane, I'm simply exhausted watching you buy the wrong things all day."

"I'm sorry," Jane said absently. "They seemed very nice to me. I feel rather pleased with them."

"But a thousand dollars is a lot of money, and the place is still only half-furnished. I don't know what John will say when he sees the few things you bought and the money all gone."

"Here's your tea," Jane said, as Gert approached with a tray. "And don't worry for John. Let him do his own worrying."

Mamie had been looking through the display window where a large white cat slept in the shade of a potted fern, and she turned suddenly and whispered, "There's that Dick fellow—that Mr. Rouston. I think he's coming in."

He did come in, and Jane realized that he must have seen them, since she well knew that the Forget-Me-Not and he had nothing in common. She saw Gert eye him with pleasure and speed up the assault on her gum.

He gave Mamie a careless nod and then asked Jane, with the charm all on, "How are you today, Mrs. Cowrer? We were sorry to hear that you were not feeling very fit last night."

Jane responded normally to her distaste for him by saying shortly that she was all right, but the next instant she forced herself to smile and invite him to sit down with them. She reminded herself, rather desperately, that she had gone to a great deal of trouble with a definite purpose in mind, and she must pursue it when the opportunity offered.

He sat down, ordered tea which he made no attempt to drink, and fell into a flow of easy talk. It was all very familiar to Jane, who had seen it so many times. He had decided that she was worthy of passing some time for him, and he was going through a regular routine. Soon he would try to date her for a cocktail or some excursion to be undertaken while her husband was at his office. She smiled back at him and hoped that she was keeping the contempt she felt for him out of her eyes.

Mamie had fallen into a silence that throbbed with suspicion and disapproval. They had called John, who was to meet them at the Forget-Me-Not and drive them home, and when at last he appeared, Mamie hailed him eagerly.

Under cover of her shouted greetings Dick took the opportunity to make the date toward which he had been aiming. Just for sherry at the hotel, at noon the following day. It was done very smoothly. He made it seem as though she had been coming into town without Mamie anyway, and might just as well have sherry with him in the cocktail lounge.

She nodded an agreement and then turned to greet John, who gave her hand a little squeeze before extending a cordial salute to Dick. Dick responded with equal cordiality and then eased himself off.

John looked after him and shook his head.

"He appears chipper enough, but it seems there's a bit of trouble.

That body they identified as his wife had no mole on her chest, and I understand there should have been one. "

CHAPTER 11

JANE'S HAND went to the collar of her coat, in a gesture of pulling it closer about her neck, and then dropped to her lap again. She should have had the mole removed. She'd have to have it done now at the earliest opportunity.

"The family must have known about the mole," Mamie said curiously. "How could they identify the body when the mole wasn't there?"

"Carelessness all around, as far as I can make out," John explained. "The family never were quite sure about that body, I believe, but they seem to have identified it on the theory that they didn't see how it could be anyone else, and they were backed up by some lazy officials who wanted the case buttoned up and removed from the unfinished business file. However, the girl's doctor saw the body and has insisted from the first that it was not Mrs. Rouston. He declares that the absence of the mole proves it, and he won't keep his mouth shut. He had some words with the family, and now they're at odds and don't speak to each other. Opinion seems to be divided among the boys in town. Some say that the body was so decomposed that it would be hard to find the mole anyway and that Dr. Zentron hated the family and is merely trying to make trouble for them."

Mamie nodded with conviction. "I'll bet that's what it is. There are always people ready and waiting to make trouble for you."

Jane longed to defend Dr. Zentron, for whom she had the greatest respect and admiration, but she forced herself to remain silent. As for the mole, there was surely no need to worry about it. Plenty of people had moles, and probably a goodly percentage of them were on the chest.

But John was thinking of that mole too. As soon as the boys had mentioned it, he had thought of Jane and of the mole on her chest. He wondered a little why she had not had it removed when she had gone to such trouble and expense over her beauty. Not that he minded it.

He liked and was fascinated by everything about Jane. But still, it would have seemed logical

On the way home in the car Mamie reminded Jane of her intention to stop in and say hello to the Roustons, but Jane decided that it was too late, and Mamie made no particular protest. She was tired, and her fatigue caused her to suggest to John that he teach Jane how to drive. "Then she can take you in every morning and pick you up in the evening, and we won't have to go pounding into town on our feet. It's a long walk."

"She'll need a learner's permit first," John explained. "She can get that tomorrow, and then I'll give her a lesson whenever she's ready."

"It won't be too difficult," Jane said carefully. "I know a little about driving. I used to drive my aunt's car occasionally."

Mamie, unable to hold it in any longer, gave John the bad news about the furniture. All the money was gone with only a few things to show for it, not nearly enough to fill all the rooms. She went on to make a few excuses for Jane, for she was afraid that John would be furious.

But John only half-listened to her. His mind was back with the leading citizens of the town. It had been a luncheon to which he was pleased to receive an invitation. Dick Rouston had not been there, and when he asked for him, he'd been given a fairly comprehensive earful. The fellow was an idle playboy, a waster who had been living on his wife's money. The wife's name had been Gloria—unsuitable, they all agreed, since she was the plain type, although she'd had nice violet-colored eyes.

Jane had violet eyes. It was one of the first things he'd ever noticed about her, the deep lovely color of her eyes.

The boys had all agreed that they liked Gloria. She was an honest, decent sort, and they were all very interested in her disappearance and the subsequent discovery of the body. The doctor was firmly of the opinion that the body was not that of Mrs. Rouston, and another man, a lawyer, declared that she had probably left because she could not stand her life with the Roustons. However, this was generally opposed by the others on the grounds that she would hardly go off and leave all her money behind. John had decided that the subject was a popular one and probably came up for discussion regularly.

Jane, who had glanced at him once or twice during his abstraction, asked, "What's the matter, John? You're very quiet."

"Nothing," he said hastily. "Just thinking."

"John's a deep one," Mamie said with pride. "He always thought a lot, even when he was a little boy."

"Then it's about time he had it all figured out," Jane murmured.

"He thought himself into being a good lawyer, didn't he?" Mamie demanded belligerently.

Jane glanced at John and saw that he was not listening to either of them, and she was suddenly frightened. Why was he so abstracted? Surely he wasn't thinking of Gloria and of herself. He mustn't—he simply must not connect them. She felt that she could not stand it if he found out.

John turned the car into the driveway, and Jane looked up at the gloomy old house. Only it didn't seem gloomy now. It was home, and somehow it was attractive. Didn't it have flowers growing on one wall of every single room?

She laughed out loud, and John looked at her quickly.

"What's so funny?"

"Oh, I was thinking about how attractive our house is, even if it is old."

"It's old all right," Mamie said, puffing a little as she climbed out of the car. "All that wooden crochet work dripping from the porch."

John took them both by the arm, and said contentedly, "Never mind the crochet work. I think it has a lot of charm and it will have a lot more charm when Jane's furnishings are delivered and arranged."

Mamie opened her mouth, but he added quickly, "And even if it is only half-furnished, it will look considerably better than if it were completely furnished with rubbish."

Mamie closed her mouth again with a snap, and Jane gave a happy little sigh. It was all right. He had stopped thinking, and she had him back again. She'd drop everything. She wouldn't keep that date with Dick.

Her mind suddenly boiled up in a rush of confused thoughts and she put her hand to her head. Of course she couldn't drop everything.

Dolly met them at the door with a broad smile. "Holy smoke!"

she said cheerfully. "Here's the master home, and not a thing in for dinner."

Mamie thrust a bag of groceries at her and snapped, "There's more coming tomorrow. Just cook that up and don't waste time talking about it."

Dolly settled the groceries comfortably on her hip, and after giving Mamie a glassy eye, she turned her attention to Jane and John.

"You got a swell wedding present in there, just come a little while ago, sent over from the big house. Ain't no use to them because they can't none of them play so much as *America* with one finger, but they heard you could play, Miz Cowrer, and the piano don't do them no good since poor Miss Gloria went, so they sent it over for you."

Jane brushed past Dolly and hurried to the living room. Why, it must be her own piano they'd sent. It must be

Her heart was pounding as she stood in the arched doorway, looking into the twilight of the huge room. Yes, there it was, gleaming against the old-fashioned, floor-length window.

She advanced a few steps, and drew in her breath sharply. They'd sent the black piano.

CHAPTER 12

JANE TOUCHED the smooth ebony of the old piano with a loving hand and was scarcely conscious of Mamie and John, who had come in behind her.

"It's not so much, is it?" Mamie said disparagingly. "Looks like an undertaker's parlor, being black that way, and it certainly is old. No wonder they didn't want it. They have a swell mahogany one in their living room, but it seems nobody plays it."

"Miss Gloria used to play," Dolly observed, joining them. "They put this piano up in the attic years ago when they bought the other one. I was only a little girl, and I remember Miss Gloria started in taking lessons. She played good too."

"It was very generous of them," John said, with a shade of annoyance in his voice, "but a bit presumptuous, I think. Why should they suppose we'd want an old thing like this? I had intended buying one of our own some time."

Jane opened the lid and softly touched the yellowed keys. She'd always loved this piano, with its darkly glowing ebony and all the elaborate carving. It needed tuning, of course, but it was in good condition. She'd always seen to that. It must be worth a good deal of money these days. It was just like them to give away a valuable old piece of furniture if they happened to feel like it. Only, why had they felt like it? Dick, of course. He was making a play for her, making dates with her behind her husband's back.

John was reading the card that had come with it. "They say you're to play it until you get your own. I presume we're expected to return it then."

"No sir," Dolly said emphatically. "Mr. Dick, he came with the van when they brought it, and he says when Mrs. Cowrer gets through with it, just throw it away. He don't want it no more."

Of course, throw it away, Jane thought bitterly. What would a lovely old thing like this mean to the Roustons? Nothing at all.

"See how it plays, Jane," Mamie suggested.

Jane sat down and began to play and lost herself at once. There were certain things which she played only on this piano because, somehow, they were right for it. She forgot John and Mamie and Dolly, and her troubled mind was soothed and peaceful. She lost all sense of time and was startled when John appeared beside her and, taking her hands, held them still.

"Time for dinner," he said, laughing at her. "And it seems that Dolly has made an utter hash of the entire meal."

It developed that Dolly had. And Mamie, although she was hungry, was well pleased.

"I wanted to help her," she said virtuously, "but that one always knows best, and nobody can tell her anything, so I left her to her own devices."

Dolly was in tears. "I bet I cooked anyway a thousand steaks in my life," she wailed, "and I never ruined one."

"Yes, you did," Mamie said cheerfully. "You ruined this one."

Jane said, "Never mind, Dolly, we all make mistakes. We'll eat it the way it is. Dry your eyes and forget about it."

Dolly dried her eyes, but she continued to make voluble apologies throughout the meal, while Mamie enjoyed herself by saying "I told you so" at intervals.

They went straight upstairs to bed after dinner, since there were no comfortable chairs in which they could sit downstairs. Jane and John established themselves with pillows and a book each, but Mamie had never been able to read in bed, so she went to sleep instead.

Jane heard Dolly slip out, cross the road, and start over the fields, which was the shortest way to her favorite tavern. Oh well, if that was what she liked—

"You're not reading," John said. "You're thinking again."

She tried to smile brightly at him and had a sensation of failure, but she said as naturally as possible, "Oh, I was putting the new furniture around the walls."

He laughed. "From what I hear, you haven't enough to go around the walls with all that thousand you spent."

"Mamie doesn't understand what I have in mind, John. As a matter of fact, I did very well. They have some surprisingly nice stuff in that shop in town."

He nodded and let a moment pass before he said rather abruptly, "I want you to get in touch with your aunt and invite her here for a visit with us."

"Oh no, she doesn't like visiting. She'd never come."

"All right," he said tolerantly, "we'll go down and visit her. I'll take a few days off."

"You mean now?" Jane asked faintly.

"Yes, now."

"But—but, John, you've just started. How can you get away?"

"I can manage it. I want to see your aunt. We'll leave tomorrow."

"Oh no," Jane said helplessly. "We can't—it's impossible. I mean she wouldn't let us in. She's the kind to send a formal invitation and then spend a week or so preparing for us."

John had been watching her, but he dropped his head back on the pillows now and stared at the ceiling. "That's what I thought you'd say," he remarked quietly.

Jane gave him a frightened glance and dropped her eyes to her book. The print blurred before them. What was it? What was he probing for, she thought desperately. He didn't suspect her, he couldn't. She simply could not stand that. If she could just get away from all the fear and trouble and start afresh with John. But it was no use. You couldn't get away from it when it was all around you. And she'd been successful so far. No one knew her. Her face was so different, and her figure too. She'd struggled and battled to put on ten pounds, and she'd kept it on too. But after all, ten pounds wasn't so much. Perhaps her figure wasn't much different.

John had taken up his book again, but he could not read it. He found himself thinking of the mole on Jane's chest and the one that had been missing from the body. Then the Rouston girl had disappeared on the same night Jane had turned up at Mamie's place. Then Jane had gone to work and changed her entire appearance. He thought of the dimple where her cheek had been pierced. That alone must have made a considerable difference in her face. Gloria Rouston was reputed to have had dark, violet-colored eyes, and so did Jane. An unusual color.

John dropped his book and stared up at the ceiling again. The whole thing was absurd, must be absurd, and yet he could not get it out of his mind. What he was suspecting would make a bigamist of Jane, and she was not like that at all. Anyway, why would she come back to this town? It seemed more likely that she'd go as far away as she could.

His imagination was running away with him. It must be. He took up his book again and made a determined effort to read, and then suddenly and quite distinctly he saw the blind man on the main street of the town, and heard his words, "Miss Gloria." *He* could not see the tremendous change in her appearance, as he had merely heard her voice.

John turned his head and looked steadily at Jane as she lay against her pillows in the adjoining bed. She was not reading. She had not turned a page in the last hour and appeared to be lost in thought.

He said suddenly into the silence, "Gloria?"

And she glanced up, still with an inward, preoccupied look, and murmured, "Yes?"

CHAPTER 13

JOHN GOT OUT of bed, put on a gown and slippers, and walked over to the window. Jane watched him, a puzzled line between her brows, and with no consciousness of having betrayed herself.

He presently turned to her and asked abruptly, "What's your game?"

She felt her body go cold. He knew, then. How had he found out? How could he possibly have found out? And what was she going to do? What could she say to him? She did not want to hurt him, and he'd have to be hurt now.

He came over and stood at the foot of her bed, and her eyes clung to him helplessly. After a moment she whispered, "What do you mean?"

"Don't waste time with that sort of nonsense," he said impatiently. "Just tell me why you did it, and what you expect to get out of it."

An ache at the back of her throat warned of impending tears, and she clenched her teeth in an effort to keep them back. When she spoke her voice was harsh, but almost steady.

"One of them pushed me over the railing of the bridge into that ravine. I must find out who it was."

"So you married me—committed bigamy—to further your own ends."

It was obvious that he did not believe that one of them had thrown her off the bridge. She got out of bed, lit a cigarette with shaking hands, and said very quietly, "John, one of them tried to murder me. I didn't want to—I couldn't go back to them. I'll admit that when I knew you were coming here, it influenced my decision to marry you. But you can believe this, too. I wish now that we could go somewhere else, that I could just live with you and never see any of them again."

It didn't appear to touch him. He said almost impersonally, "I believe you need medical attention."

She had a moment of utter despair. So John thought she was unbalanced too. They all did. Perhaps she was. Anger flamed up in her, and she turned on him furiously.

"It's very easy to solve the whole thing by deciding that I'm mentally unbalanced. That's what the others would have done if I'd gone back to them. It would be a simple, comfortable solution for everyone, except myself. I *know* I was pushed over that railing, deliberately, and I'm damned if I see why I should take it lying down. I intend to find out which one of them did it. As for you, I had no idea of marrying you in the beginning. You'll remember that I refused the first time you asked me. But then you asked me again—"

"And it occurred to you that it would be very convenient, after all," he supplied flatly.

"Oh, John, no!" The tears came then. She could not stop them. She put her arm across her eyes, childishly, and heard John walk out of the room.

She cried for a long time, stretched out on the bed with her head buried in the pillows. She had held herself in for so long, walking on a tightrope, terrified of making a wrong move, burning night and day with a deep anger that must be kept locked up within herself. The tears, now that they had come, were a tremendous relief, and she let them flow. She heard John come in once or twice and go out again, but she did not move until at last the paroxysm was over. She realized then that she had a violent headache and that her eyes were swollen nearly shut. She dragged herself off the bed and went to the bathroom, where she took some aspirin and bathed her face in cold water. She went back to bed and, resting her head against the pillows, lit a cigarette and stared into space, thinking of nothing.

John came in after awhile and silently handed her a cup of black coffee. She took it gratefully and drank it down, although it wasn't very hot. John sat on the other bed, smoking and waiting for her to finish.

She knew that he'd made up his mind to some course of action, and because anger still stirred in her, she turned on him first.

"You need not bother telling me when to go to the doctor, and what doctor, and that it won't hurt, because I am not going to any doctor."

"Entirely up to you," he said easily. "It could hardly concern me. I'm only the sucker in the background."

She had been prepared for an argument and suddenly found herself with nothing left to say. She put the cup on the bedside table with a slight clatter and lit another cigarette.

John stirred and asked, "What do you intend to do when you find out who pushed you over the bridge?"

Out of a rather heavy silence she said at last, "I don't really know. I suppose it will depend on the circumstances."

He nodded. "I'm in a somewhat difficult position, because I can't afford a fancy scandal just now. As far as I'm concerned, you can go ahead with the sleuthing, always keeping an open mind, I hope. But there's one thing I'm going to insist upon. If you do make a discovery, you're to do nothing whatever about it. Do you understand?"

"What do you mean?

"I mean that you are to come and tell me, and no one else. You can look upon me as your legal adviser."

"And if I decide to do it my way?"

His eyes narrowed a little, and he said quietly, "Then we'll wash it up right now. You'll pack your things and return to your own home."

Jane shivered and closed her eyes for a moment. "I'll do it your way," she said faintly.

"Right. Now tomorrow move one of these beds into another room and make up a suitable story to tell Mamie."

She nodded, and he pulled a blanket from his bed and went out of the room. She watched him, wondering in an exhausted fashion where he was going to sleep. There were no couches, no beds, nothing. There was a window seat in the bay window of the dining room, but it would be hard and cold and drafty.

She moved her head restlessly on the pillows and gave way to a bitter attack of conscience. How could she have done this thing, pretended to marry a man and spent over a thousand dollars of his money on furniture, just to further her own ends. She was worse than her own family, who at least had taken her money openly and without any false pretenses.

The pain in her head pounded dully through the aspirin and she thought, in sudden exasperation, that he was being a bit melodramatic, anyway. After all, they'd shared a bedroom for so long that one more night could hardly matter, especially when it was a cold night with only a window seat available. But then, perhaps he simply couldn't stand the sight of her any more and didn't want to be near her. That was far worse than her first realization that the family couldn't stand the sight of her. John mattered a great deal more than any of them. The thought of losing him was so sharply painful that she thrust it away quickly. Somehow, it would work out. It must.

The house was very quiet, except for an occasional creaking of old woodwork. Suddenly she was sitting straight up in bed, her ears straining against the pounding of her heart.

Downstairs the piano was playing very softly.

CHAPTER 14

WHO COULD BE playing the piano in that vast, dim empty room in the middle of the night? Not John nor Mamie, for neither of them could play. Dolly—it must be Dolly. She might have come home drunk. But she had never seen Dolly drunk in all the years she had known her. She would go to her tavern and apparently spend a hilarious evening, but she was always sober when she came home.

The soft, faraway melody ceased and did not start again, and Jane peered nervously at the clock. It was nearly five. Perhaps she had imagined the piano, but that would mean that everybody was right in thinking her a mental case. She ought to go downstairs now and see if anyone were there.

She got out of bed, shaking with cold and nervousness, and put on slippers and a warm robe. These old houses were always cold. It was impossible to heat them properly. The furnace should be kept going at full blast all night. She'd speak to John about it. Only John wouldn't listen to her now. Probably he wouldn't ever want to talk to her again.

There was a sharp creak from the stairs, but she forced herself to leave the room and go out into the hall. The stairs were always creaking, whether anyone walked on them or not. She went down slowly, clutching her robe tightly around her and with her heart pounding. The piano was in the drawing room. You had to call it the drawing room in a house like this. There was a library opposite, with the dining room behind it and an immense kitchen at the rear of the house.

Jane crossed the wide hall and came to a sudden stop when she saw that the sliding doors of the drawing room were closed. They had not been closed earlier, she knew. In fact, she had never seen them closed at all.

Perhaps John was in there, only that would be silly of him. The dining room was warmer and had the window seat. She put tentative hands on the two doors and eased them apart, and to her surprise they rolled back smoothly, as though they had been oiled recently. But of course Dolly must have done it. Dolly was an efficient handyman around the house, far more efficient at things of this sort than she had ever been at cooking and cleaning.

The room stretched out before her, empty, silent, and dark, except for a streak of moonlight that lay across the piano. She moved closer and saw that the lid was closed over the keys as she had left it earlier. She stood for a moment, surrounded by darkness and silence, and then the story of the melancholy spirit who came here to play the piano suddenly slid into her mind. She gave a little gasp, and her courage deserted her. She turned and fled from the room.

Back in her bedroom she got into bed again and lay huddled under the blankets, her whole body shaking in an explosion of nerves. She must be mental, she thought wildly, if a silly ghost story could send her into a sweat of terror. Only it wasn't mental. It was natural. Anyone would be scared in such a combination of circumstances. She mustn't start thinking of herself as deranged or she'd be lost.

Her body began slowly to relax, and she presently fell into a heavy sleep of utter exhaustion.

Mamie woke her late in the morning with a cheerful greeting and a breakfast tray.

"If I'd let you go on, I think you'd have slept the day away. Besides, your furniture just came, and I don't know how you want it arranged."

Jane took the tray onto her lap and found that she felt curiously relaxed and almost peaceful. She had for so long been in fear of John discovering her secret that there was relief in the blow having fallen. She ate her breakfast with an appetite and was kept from thinking too much by Mamie, who bounced in and out of the room with questions about the furniture. Once she paused long enough to say, "You look like the wrath of God. And what's the matter with your eyes? They're all puffed up. John said you were sick."

Jane shrugged, but before she could think up an answer, Mamie had gone flying off again. She finished her breakfast and had a leisurely cigarette. She felt depleted enough to have stayed in bed all day, but loud noises from all over the house warned her that Mamie was arranging the furniture and that she had better go out and join the fray.

She bathed and dressed in a bit of a hurry, and then went down to view Mamie's handiwork. Everything had been placed cater-cornered, and Mamie explained defensively that the arrangement made the rooms look less bare. Jane went to work at once, rearranging, setting things against the walls, and trying to use enough tact so that Mamie's feelings would not be hurt.

When there was barely enough time to keep it, she remembered her date with Dick. The thing was bitterly distasteful to her, but she grimly prepared herself to go out and was relieved when Mamie decided that the long walk to town would be too much.

Just before she left Jane asked Mamie, and felt decidedly foolish in asking, whether she had heard the piano playing in the small hours of the morning.

Mamie gave her an odd look. "The piano? Playing in the night? Of course not. You've been having nightmares. I told you you looked like the wreck of the Hesperus this morning."

Now *she* thinks I'm crazy, Jane thought as she started off. But she *had* heard that piano. She'd heard it distinctly. The melody had been familiar to her and yet, try as she would, she could not put a name to it. Well, no wonder she could not remember things, if she were as weak in the head as everyone seemed to think.

She straightened her shoulders and began to walk briskly. As she approached the skating pond she glanced over and saw two figures swinging along on the smooth surface. Betsy and Pete Hoge again.

Jane felt a spasm of anger. Why didn't her family look after the girl? And why wasn't she in school? She'd been wanting to quit school for some long time past, but surely Rose and Dick had not allowed it. What was the matter with them, anyway? She'd have to try to let them know about Pete Hoge. If they knew the girl was fooling around

with him they ought certainly to put a stop to it. Why wasn't he working in the morning? He was supposed to be a salesman of some sort,
but she could not remember what he sold.

She was chilled and tired by the time she reached the cocktail bar,
and she found Dick waiting for her, looking sulky. She discovered that
his annoyance was caused by the fact that Rose, with a man in tow,
had attached herself to him and was not to be shaken off.

Dick introduced them, perforce, and Jane, with Betsy on her mind,
was so annoyed with Rose that she had to force a smile onto her face.
She did not catch the man's name, but it developed that he was the
manager of the hotel and a newcomer to town. They called him Bub.

Bub was good-looking and had a lively tongue. Jane tried to keep
up with their nonsense, but in the end the other three were making all
the smart and funny remarks, and she found her face aching with the
effort to laugh gaily and naturally at them. She wanted to yawn and
had to hold her jaw rigid to combat it.

In the midst of the hilarity Rose turned to her suddenly and said,
"Do you know, my Aunt Sally and I saw you around town yesterday,
and we could both swear that we've seen you somewhere before."

CHAPTER 15

JANE STRETCHED a smile across her face in a rather frightened
exhibition of her new teeth. She did not say anything, since nothing
occurred to her.

"We decided in the end," Rose said comfortably, "that we must
have met you, or at least seen you, at some resort."

"Perhaps," Jane murmured noncommittally.

"I haven't seen her anywhere before," Dick said, smiling into her
eyes. "I'd have remembered her."

Bub leaned across the table and asked, "How do you like small-
town life, Mrs. Cowrer?"

Jane considered the question gravely, as Gloria might have done,
but before she could answer, Rose said impatiently, "Don't be silly,
Bub—such a fatuous question." She took a small, glittering compact
from her bag and delicately touched the tiny pink puff to her nose and

chin. She studied portions of her face in the shining little mirror with deadly concentration and then suddenly snapped the thing shut and dropped it back into her bag.

Jane had winced, as usual, during the course of this public repair job, but at second thought it prompted her to pull out her own compact and follow suit. She must remember to be as different as possible in every way. Here was Dick sitting directly beside her, his quick eyes missing nothing, his shrewd mind usually ahead of her slower, deeper intelligence.

Rose idly ran her white, well-groomed fingers up and down the stem of her glass and after a moments silence said to Jane, "I think your husband is perfectly precious. Do you mind if I flirt with him just a little bit?"

Jane was surprised at the sudden fury which boiled up within her, but she managed to say flippantly, "Go as far as you can."

Dick glanced at her and grinned. "No *Bon Ami* in that one. I think it scratched a bit."

Rose made a face at him and gave Jane's hand a little pat. "I'll take up your challenge, honey, and see what I can do."

Jane dropped her hands into her lap and took a quick breath. "I've seen your daughter twice in the morning, skating on the pond. She's a lovely girl. You must be very proud of her."

Rose shrugged on a vexed little sigh. "She's pretty enough, but she plagues me to death. I can't get her to put her mind on anything but the boys."

"It wasn't a boy who was with her on the pond. It was a man who appeared to be a good deal older than she is. I thought he might be an uncle, but John's aunt, who was with me, said he was a Mr. Hoge."

Rose laughed. "Oh yes, Pete. He's been a close friend of the family for years. He might just as well be her uncle."

She seemed utterly unconcerned, and Jane fretted over a desire to tell her that Pete was looking at Betsy in a way no uncle should, but somehow she couldn't. Instead, she asked, "Where does she go to school?"

Rose looked a trifle mortified. "Well, she flunked out of the local high school. So stupid. She'd have had to spend another year in the same class, you see, and watch all her friends go on, and of course

she didn't want that. Anyway, the high school here is no place for
Betsy, so I shall pack her off to a girls' school next fall. I couldn't get
her in this fall, but she's had some tutoring during the winter. Only I
wish I could get her to study a little."

Jane dropped her eyes and tried to relax her compressed lips.
They'd always wanted to send the girl to a finishing school, and now
they were going to do it. But there was no need for Betsy to have
flunked out of her class. She was perfectly able to keep abreast of her
studies if she wanted to.

Dick put his hand on her arm and asked lightly, "What now? You are
always retreating into some far-off place where we can't follow you."

That was too typical of Gloria, and Jane, brought back sharply,
began to babble.

"The piano—I've been wanting to thank you. I was so terrifically
thrilled when I came home and found it standing there by the window.
I really don't know what to say to you or how to express my grati-
tude. But I can't accept such a gift. I must pay for it—"

"Not a penny," Rose said firmly. "It belonged to Dick's wife, you
know, and it reminds us of her too much. She was very fond of it. As
soon as we heard that you played, we felt that you must have it." She
turned her head away and was silent for a moment while two tears
formed at the corners of her eyes. She brushed them away and murmured, "Poor Gloria. She'd be glad to know that someone is playing
her piano."

Jane stared down at her drink. Poor Gloria. Yes, and poor Jane
too, and poor John. It was a pity she hadn't died, since she brought
nothing but trouble to people. A wave of self-pity engulfed her, and
she felt her eyes welling with tears. She must think of something else
quickly, before the others noticed. Mamie. At least she had been good
to Mamie, and Mamie really needed her. Instead of spending the winter on someone's couch in the city, she had a room of her own, with
the bureau across the corner the way she liked it.

Rose was saying, "Have you a date with your husband for lunch,
Mrs. Cowrer?"

"Call her Jane," Dick said lazily. "That's her name."

"Yes, please call me Jane. And I'm not having lunch with my husband."

"You really ought to," Rose murmured. "He's far too attractive for you to let him float around loose."

"You go and have lunch with him then," Dick suggested. "Jane is lunching with me."

"This guy is making me jealous before I ever see him," Bub said aggrievedly. "Listen, Rose——"

But Rose had let out a little shriek and was waving her hand wildly in the air. "Speak of the devil—there he is! John! Hi, John!"

Jane turned her head quickly and saw him. He was with another man and was looking rather uncertainly in Rose's direction. Rose went over to him and, clutching his hand, led him back to where the others were sitting. She completely ignored his companion, who was bald and looked respectable.

John appeared to be slightly annoyed. He was obviously surprised to see Jane, and she said "Hello" in a small voice. Rose introduced him to Bub, and Bub, after a brief nod, observed, "You seem to have taken my girlfriend's eye, although I can't see it myself."

John didn't know what he was talking about, and asked rather impatiently, "Where's Bert?"

"Bert has passed out of your life," Rose said firmly, "at least for the present." She gestured across the room to where the bald, respectable man was now sitting at a table with some other people, studying a menu.

"Probably they expect John to eat along with them," Bub suggested hopefully.

"We expect him to eat along with us," Rose declared. "Get things started, Bub."

John capitulated, after warning them that he had only twenty minutes, and Bub got things started by hailing a busy waiter and peremptorily demanding menus, followed immediately by lunch. He seemed completely unconcerned about the other diners.

Once the lunch had been ordered he found that he had nothing to do, since Rose was completely absorbed in John, and Dick was leaning toward Jane and talking to her in a low voice. But Bub had never been a man to be easily discouraged, and after one competent glance at the situation he decided to horn in on Jane and Dick. Jane realized at once that he was smooth, quite as smooth as Dick in his own way, and she began to have a curious feeling of being torn limb from limb. She gave up at last, and putting on a stiff smile tried to listen to Rose and John.

John seemed to be giving thanks for the piano, and Bub, seeing that Jane's attention had strayed, turned around and listened too. He presently put on a superior little smile and observed with a certain amount of malice, "Don't be too impressed with that gift. It was getting on the Roustons' nerves. The spirit of Dick's wife had been drifting in and playing on it during the night."

CHAPTER 16

JANE GAVE A little gasp and was silent, her eyes wide on Bub's face.

Rose said, "Oh, Bub! For heaven's sake!" But Dick, tapping a cigarette on the table, frowned and looked rather serious.

"It's true enough," he said slowly. "It gave me the creeps. Every now and then it would play, apparently by itself. Did it perform last night in its new surroundings?"

John laughed shortly. "Not a sound, but then perhaps we're not sufficiently imaginative."

Jane looked down into her glass and decided to say nothing. Apparently John had not heard the piano playing. After all, the sliding doors had been closed, and he had presumably spent the night in the dining room. Mamie apparently had not heard it, either, but it seemed likely that it had something to do with the hot-air heating system. The register in her room evidently picked up sounds from the drawing room. Only, who was playing the piano? Someone must be doing it, unless she really was insane. But they had heard it in the other house, too, so there must be some reasonable explanation.

Lunch was brought in, and she ate mechanically, her mind so far away that ten minutes later she had no idea of what the menu had been.

John glanced up at her once and said, "I thought you were going to stay at home today and arrange the furniture."

"I'm going back right after lunch," she replied confusedly. "I—I'll do it then."

"Oh, nonsense!" Rose cried gaily. "You can arrange furniture any time. Such a boring occupation! Let's play some bridge."

Jane said, "No!" and sounded almost shocked. It seemed all wrong to sit around in the middle of the day playing bridge when there were so many serious and important things to do.

"You'll play, won't you, John?" Rose asked in a wheedling voice.

John shook his head. "Have to get back," he said briefly. Jane realized that she should have agreed to the plan, and murmured doubtfully, "I'd like to play, but I must go home for at least half an hour. Perhaps after that —"

Dick said, "Good!" and stood up. "I'll drive you out, wait for you, and drive you back. Let's go."

He helped Jane to her feet with a hand under her elbow, and they walked out while John looked after them, seething with impotent fury. He hated seeing her go off with that man, who was legally her husband, but there was nothing he could do about it. He'd simply have to face facts and pick up the pieces. He needed to get her out of his mind as soon as possible and see what he could do about moving away from this town. Unfortunately, it could not be managed just now, and in the meantime he'd better try to take an interest in other women. He turned back to Rose, who still sat beside him, and she immediately ordered Bub to go and prepare a place for them to play bridge.

Bub went, but he was in a bad temper. He knew that she was sending him off so that she could be alone with the lawyer fellow, and he muttered through clenched teeth and with narrowed eyes that he'd be damned if she was going to get away with it. He had always played fast and loose with his own wife, from whom he was now separated, but he had no intention of being pushed around himself. He made a mental resolution to this effect three times while he superintended the setting up of a bridge table and the accompanying equipment.

John, left with Rose, found himself relaxing in her attractive company over a few drinks. He felt that it was what he needed, and yet he was unable to stay away from the subject of Gloria.

Rose didn't seem to mind talking about her. "A very fine type of person, really," she said thoughtfully, "but dull, you know—terribly.

She was clever, of course, but school clever, and she and Dick were a bad match. I know perfectly well that everyone thinks he married her for her money, but actually it isn't true. Dick was always easygoing about money. He didn't care whether he had it or not, and he was always able to get along well enough without it. Not many people know this, but Dick really fell in love with Gloria's eyes."

"Her eyes?" John repeated, looking down rather somberly at his drink.

"Her eyes were a very unusual color, a sort of deep violet, really lovely. It's just like Dick, of course. He was always given to tremendous enthusiasms, and this, time it was Gloria's eyes. First thing he knew, he was married to her."

"And then he began to regret it," John suggested.

"Yes, and you couldn't really blame him. She wouldn't let him alone. Wanted him to work his young life away in jobs that were unsuitable. You know the sort of thing. Certainly Dick goes from job to job, but we all know that he'll land on his feet eventually."

John nodded with a certain amount of reserve and asked without much interest, "What is he doing now?"

"Oh, he's between jobs right now," Rose said brightly. "He's taking his time and waiting for the right thing, which is so much better, I always think, than getting into something and then not being satisfied."

"I suppose," John murmured tolerantly, "that his wife's death was very upsetting, and that must have held him back."

"Yes, of course," Rose agreed eagerly. "And then the fact that they were not getting on too well somehow made it worse."

John was unable to follow that line of reasoning but let it go without comment. After a short silence he said thoughtfully, "I don't see how it was that no one heard her fall. Wouldn't she have screamed?"

Rose drew her brows together in a delicate little frown. "Why, I suppose she must have, but the waterfall is fairly noisy, and the house in which we were staying was some distance away."

"But didn't you miss her that night?"

Rose was getting bored with the conversation and managed to make it obvious by the inflection of her voice and a faint movement of her shoulders.

"No one ever dreamed of waiting around for Gloria. It wasn't to be expected. She loved to ramble off into the moonlight, and the rest of us hated it. Imagine—all the mosquitoes, and perhaps snakes underfoot. Anyway, we all went to bed and didn't discover that she was missing until the next morning."

"What about Dick?" John persisted. "Didn't they sleep in the same room?"

Rose laughed. "They had to, up there, because the place wasn't large enough to have it otherwise, although they had separate rooms at home. But Dick's bed was in one corner of that room and hers in the other. He'd had a few drinks, and he went straight into a heavy sleep. I suppose, if he thought about it at all, he assumed she'd come back and was in her bed."

John nodded, and Rose made a restless movement. "May I have another cocktail?" she asked prettily.

He glanced up at her. "No. You've had too many now for the middle of the day."

She pouted, and John added, "I'll buy you an ice-cream cone, if you like."

Rose gave a little scream. "What a perfectly horrid suggestion!"

John looked at his wristwatch and muttered, "Shouldn't they be back by now?"

Rose gave him an odd little smile and said, "Don't be silly."

An instant later her expression changed to one of faint annoyance, and he looked up to see Sally, slim and well-groomed, with her gold hair and dark eyes that were almost wine-colored. She was, John decided, older than she looked. In spite of the difference in age and coloring, there was something reminiscent of Jane about her, and when Rose murmured without enthusiasm, "Hello, Sally," he remembered that this was the aunt.

John rose, and Sally said, "I can't stay. I'm my way to do some shopping, if you can call it shopping in this Godforsaken place."

She went her way, and Rose, watching her out of sight, murmured more to herself than John, "She'll have to lengthen that dress a bit."

There was a little silence, and then Rose suddenly waved her hand in the air and called shrilly, "Hi, Allison!"

John looked up to see a girl crossing the lobby, a glamorous blonde young thing with a self-conscious swing to her hips.

"She didn't see me," Rose said, as the girl passed out of sight.

"Who is she?" John asked idly.

Rose had her lipstick out and was delicately touching up her lips. "Allison? She's Dick's fiancée."

CHAPTER 17

JOHN TOOK a neatly folded handkerchief from his pocket and mopped his forehead. This was awful, he thought rather wildly. Something would have to be done. He couldn't simply stand to one side and let Dick marry the girl.

"When are they planning to be married?" he asked heavily.

"In June. Allison wants a large wedding, and Dick is quite agreeable, so they're really going to make a splash."

"She has plenty of money, then?" John asked, and felt uncomfortably that his question was impertinent.

Rose raised her shoulders in a delicate little shrug and said, "Not a dime. But her father is so far in debt now that he might as well give her a big wedding as not."

"I see." John realized that Rose was quite in sympathy with this line of reasoning, which was completely opposed to his own method of spending only what you had in hand, and not all of that. But he was conscious of a distinct sense of relief. If the marriage were not until June, there would surely be time to untangle the knotted problem first, and he need not say anything for the present. He'd have to work fast, though. It was first necessary to establish whether Jane were mentally unbalanced or whether one of these people really had pushed her over that bridge.

"Is Miss Allison a newcomer here?" he asked.

"Newcomer?" Rose said vaguely. "Oh, no. Allison Ketria has lived here all her life. Actually, she and Betsy are friends, but she's several years older than Betsy. Smooth, isn't she?"

"Very. I should judge that she'll make Dick a much better wife than the first one."

Rose nodded. "It will be a much more suitable marriage. She'll fit right in with us, and we're really looking forward to having her."

"You all have a lot of fun, don't you?" John asked, smiling at her.

"Why not?"

"Of course. But I can't help wondering why *you* don't marry again. I should have thought someone would have worn down your resistance by now." He felt impertinent again, but he was driven by the pressing need to know all about this family that he could possibly uncover.

Rose gave him a little half-smile that acknowledged the implied compliment, and then the smile faded rather suddenly.

"You've lost your faith in marriage?"

"No—no, of course not. It's perfectly all right—"

John could see that she was not to be enticed further on this subject, so he let it drop. Probably it had nothing to do with the truth for which he was so earnestly probing in any case. He presently left her to go back to his office, his mind fretting over the fact that Jane and Dick had not yet returned.

Jane had placed Dick in the drawing room, on their arrival at her house, and asked him to wait until she came down again. Upstairs, she enlisted Mamie's help and managed to get John's bed shifted into another room. Mamie willingly gave two vigorous arms and a strong back to the job, but she was dead against the whole thing and said so, not once but several times.

"John must have his proper sleep," Jane kept saying, quietly but firmly. "He works hard and needs his rest. I sleep badly. I toss around and have nightmares, and it disturbs him."

"Let him get used to it," Mamie protested. "It's his duty as a husband to get used to those things."

Jane said, "No," and then heard a step behind her, and whirled around to find that Dick had joined them. He was bland with offers to help in moving the furniture, but Jane burned with a fury which she was obliged to conceal. She accepted his help as graciously as possible and averted her eyes from the faint smile that appeared on his face when he understood the significance of the new arrangement.

"It's much better all around," he said easily. "Gives husband and wife more privacy and a little personal freedom."

"And paves the way to a divorce," Mamie snapped.

When the change was completed, Jane and Dick drove back to
the hotel. They found Rose and Bub waiting in a small writing room
where the bridge table had been set up.

It was amazing to Jane, as it always had been to Gloria, how
these gay, shallow people could become suddenly deadly serious at
the bridge table. During the playing of a hand they observed a sacred
silence, and the shuffling and dealing period was usually given over to
a discussion of the previous hand. Occasionally, however, snatches of
extraneous conversation crept in, and Rose presently introduced one
of these by saying, "Allison was here a little while ago, Dick."

He said, "Really? I didn't know she was back."

"Well, you know it now."

He nodded. "So I know it now. Next time I'm dummy, I'll go and
phone."

He was dummy almost immediately, and when he had left, Jane
asked, "Who's Allison?" knowing full well that it must be Allison Ketria.

"Dick's fiancée," Rose said, a shadow of a frown indicating her
impatience at the interruption.

Jane's entire hand fell to the floor, and she was able to hide her
shock and confusion in the resulting scuffle to pick up the cards. When
peace had been restored, she asked faintly, "When are they being
married?"

"June," Rose said briefly. She apparently had a problem, and took
so long to study her hand that Jane had time to recover her compo-
sure and decide, as John had done, that the whole thing would surely
be settled in some way by June.

Dick came back and sat down. When the hand was over, he said,
"She was not at home."

Rose finished writing the score and pushed the pad and pencil
away with a petulant motion. "Of course not. She was in the lobby a
little while ago. Why would she run home?"

"To wait for my phone call," Dick said and picked up his hand.
But his concentration on the game had been disturbed, and he was
obviously uneasy. Jane wondered a little about him. He had always
been so casual with women. They had had to run after him. But of
course Allison was the same way—the boys had always run after her.
Perhaps Dick was actually in love with the girl this time.

She had a moment of vertigo when the cards blurred before her eyes. She was a little frightened and decided to make a strong effort to put the whole thing out of her mind, at least for a while. Certainly it would not help matters if she became ill.

They were suddenly and breezily interrupted by Aunt Sally, who walked in smoking a cigarette in a silver-and-black holder, with her odd, wine-colored eyes full of mischief. She and Jane were introduced, and Sally was told that she must behave herself and not interrupt the game.

She said, "Phooey!" and sat down close to the table. After fidgeting with a heavy silver bracelet that banded her left wrist, she observed, "I can't stay long, anyway. I still have some errands, but I need a rest."

She was quiet for awhile after that, and Jane ceased to notice her and began to think about Allison and Dick again. If Dick were really in love with that girl, why was he making dates with Jane? It was a disturbing thought, somehow, but she tried to brush it away by reflecting that Dick was the type to try to date anyone who took his eye, no matter how his emotions might be tied up.

Sally got up from her chair and began to move around restlessly. She did not say anything, but when Dick started to play a hand she looked first at his cards and then hurried around to see what the others held.

Dick put his hand face down on the table and gave her a cold eye. "Sally! Either you'll sit quietly in your chair or you'll go on about your business."

"Why, I haven't said one word," she protested shrilly. "And I'm keeping an absolutely poker face. I don't see what you're objecting to."

"I'm objecting, no doubt, because I'm a fussy, unreasonable stupe, but I'm still objecting."

Sally pouted. "When it comes to bridge you are a fussy, unreasonable stupe. You'd think the fate of the world depended on a pack of silly cards."

"We'll grant everything you say," Dick told her. "But run away, now, and buy a new hat, will you? And I'll mix you an extra-special cocktail tonight."

Sally didn't appear to have heard him. She had caught sight of Mamie wending her way through the lobby, and she made a face which relaxed into a giggle and murmured, "Murder!".

Mamie found them in the writing room and greeted them all with a cheerful grin, including Bub, who was still a stranger to her. Bub found it a little hard to endure. He gazed off into space with a look of agony and drummed his fingers on the table.

Mamie blew her nose vigorously on a yellow-and-green hand-kerchief, and then tucked it into her bosom. "I might have known it would be bridge," she declared heartily. "It's worse than booze for some people. Here's our bride with a whole house to fix up, and she sits playing bridge all the afternoon."

"How did you get into town, Mamie?" Jane asked, feeling embarrassed.

"Oh, I just—er—windy out, isn't it?"

Jane realized that she must have thumbed her way in and fell silent.

Sally, who had always been a kindly soul at heart, finally took pity on the bridge players and led Mamie away.

The game progressed quietly for some time after that until Jane, glancing up from an absorbing hand, saw that John was standing at the door, watching them. She was frightened again and wondered whether he intended to expose her now, in front of them all.

He held her eye for a moment and then advanced into the room and said quietly, "I'm ready to take you home, Jane."

Dick glanced up and murmured, "Right away. We've just finished." He turned to Jane and put his hand over hers. "It's an odd thing, my dear, but your bridge game is very much like the way my wife played."

CHAPTER 18

JANE FELT THE shock right out to the ends of her fingers and toes. It was the way he had said it, and the look in his eyes. He knew.

She pulled her hand away as though it had been burned and stood up abruptly. Dick finished adding up the score, and they settled their losses and winnings.

John said, "Come on, Jane, Mamie is waiting in the lobby."

She pulled on her coat and gloves, said good-by to them all, and went out into the lobby with her head whirling. Mamie was there, talking volubly to Sally, and Sally was listening intently. Jane was instantly apprehensive. She knew that Sally would be showing signs of restlessness and boredom if the tale were merely a history of Mamie's life, but Sally was obviously interested, and therefore it must be something else. Something about herself, perhaps, so that Sally could put two and two together. But that was silly. She must not start imagining that everyone knew about her. Dick knew, though.

She turned to John and heard herself saying, "He knows. I'm sure of it."

"Who?" John asked sharply.

"Dick."

"Why? Just because he said you played bridge like his wife?"

Jane nodded, her eyes on his face.

"Nonsense! It was a natural enough comment. Of course you play like his wife."

But Jane shook her head. "It was the way he had said it, and the look in his eyes."

John put his arm around Mamie and smiled at Sally. "Do you mind if we carry her off? I expect dinner is ready and waiting at home, and although Mamie would rather talk than eat, I'm a working man and need to be nourished at regular intervals."

Sally sparkled a smile and told John that it was a mean thing to do, but since she was only a weak woman she'd give in gracefully. She accompanied them out to the sidewalk, talking and laughing with John all the way, and then found that it was too cold out there. She made a little face at Jane, and said, "Aren't men inconsiderate? He keeps me out here talking while I freeze to death."

Jane assumed a smile, which was wasted on Sally, as she had already flown back inside, but John noticed it. "Better take it off," he said dryly. "It might crack the face."

Jane took it off and decided simply to look blank in the future when she wasn't actually amused. The forced smile was becoming too much of an effort, and showed it.

Mamie, settling into the back seat of the car, said, "I wish you'd get that learner's permit, or whatever it is, Jane. I got sort of embarrassed coming in this afternoon."

"What happened?"

"Well." Mamie extracted the yellow-and-green handkerchief from her bosom and then put it back again without using it. "As a matter of fact, I was walking along, and I heard a car and just stuck my thumb up without looking."

John said, "Mamie! For God's sake!"

"Now don't start fussing," Mamie protested. "You always were a prim little boy. You used to drive me crazy. Insisting on my finding a men's room for you, when there were the wide-open spaces. But anyway, what I was telling you—this car stopped for me, only it wasn't a car, exactly, but a small truck. I couldn't send him away after thumbing him like that, so I had to get in."

"What sort of a truck?" John asked, in a voice of long suffering.

"It was perfectly clean. I mean, it wasn't garbage, or anything. Just a man selling eggs from his farm. He was a very nice man, quite interesting, only he *would* deliver me right to the door of the hotel. It was a bit embarrassing, but what could I do about it?"

"Mamie," John said grimly, "do you realize that I am trying to become one of the town's leading citizens? Will you, for God's sake, take a taxi the next time you want to go in to town? I shall be more than glad to pay for it."

"Listen to him!" Mamie jeered shrilly. "Imagine me spending your hard-earned money, John Cowrer, on taxis, of all things. The egg man is a decent citizen, and the town's leading lawyer shouldn't be such a stuffed shirt that he won't allow his aunt to associate with the poor but honest."

"How do you know he's honest?" John asked. "And for that matter, how do you know he's poor? For all you know, you may have been cavorting around in the truck of a rich crook."

"I did not cavort," said Mamie weakly. She was silent for a while, and then she murmured, "Just imagine, I never thought of him being rich and dishonest. Of course you never know these days, what with the workers switching places with the white-collar gang."

Jane giggled, and it was such an unusual sound from her that both Mamie and John turned to look at her.

Dinner was ready when they reached the house, and it was a much better meal this time. It developed, however, that Mamie had prepared most of the dishes earlier in the afternoon, and Dolly had only to warm them later on.

But Mamie had something else on her mind. As soon as Dolly had left the room she turned to John and said earnestly, "You're making a big mistake to let your wife sleep in a separate room. No matter how she tosses around at night or yells out in a nightmare, it's your duty to get used to it. Separate rooms are the first steps to a divorce."

John gave her a cold, level stare, and said, "We won't discuss it, Mamie."

She subsided, but she mumbled something which ended in, "and you'll see that I'm right."

Jane felt a little sorry for her and created a diversion by asking if she knew of Dick's engagement.

"Him engaged? Why, I can't believe it. Who's the girl?"

Dolly, who had come in with the coffee, obligingly supplied the answer. "It's this here Allison Ketria. She's marrying him for his money. Everybody knows that. Or maybe *he* don't. He thinks all the dames fall for him. She's pretty, I'll give her that, but I'll bet she wouldn't want no one poking into her diary."

"Dolly." John did no more than pronounce her name, and she skipped back into the kitchen looking guilty and embarrassed.

Jane wondered a little about her. She had never known her to speak so freely, and at last she came to the conclusion that she was being goaded by Mamie. Jane had never used any special voice or manner for any servant and as a result had always been respected by them. Mamie, she decided, was too anxious to make sure that Dolly realized their respective positions.

After dinner Mamie insisted that John go upstairs and inspect his new bedroom. She lamented that both bedrooms were now spoiled because the furniture had to be divided between them, but John looked rather forbidding again, so she did not pursue it any further.

Both Jane and John were uninterested now in the house, which had gone so wrong for them, and Mamie was disappointed when they retired early to their separate bedrooms.

Jane was tired, and she went to bed and to sleep almost immediately. Later, she opened her eyes on the darkness with an indefinable feeling that she had been asleep for some hours.

It was the piano again. The faint, faraway melody seeped into the room and seemed to float up against the shadowy walls. Jane lay and listened, her body rigid and her hands clenched at her sides. It stopped after a while, rather abruptly, and she waited tensely for some time, but there was no further sound.

She switched on the bedside light and, after a moment or two to rally her courage, got up and put on a warm robe and slippers. It was cold out in the hall, and she drew the robe more tightly around her scared, shivering body. She touched the switch at the head of the stairs that lighted the lower hall and forced herself to go down, although she wanted only to run back to her room and hide her head under the blankets.

The sliding doors were closed, but they moved easily under her clammy fingers, and she peered fearfully into the long, dark room. She could see that there was no one sitting at the piano, and after a moment's hesitation she advanced a few steps and switched on the light.

Allison Ketria lay almost at her feet, her lovely blond head in a pool of blood.

CHAPTER 19

THE GIRL'S DEAD face looked almost peaceful. The eyes were open, and the soft, gold hair drifted across the still forehead. Jane knew that she was dead and yet heard her own voice saying frantically, "Allison! Allison!"

After a minute or two her brain began to function more reasonably, and she knew that she must get help. She turned and fled up the stairs, her breath coming short and hard. She went straight to John's room and flung open the door, and as she approached the bed and the comfort of his support, she broke into dry sobbing.

John heaved up in the bed and switched on a lamp. His eyes were still heavy with sleep, and he looked at her with a sort of confused irritation.

"It's that girl," Jane stammered, "that Allison. She's lying down there in the drawing room, and I—I think she's dead."

John got out of bed at once and put on a robe. "Where did you say? In the drawing room?"

Jane nodded mutely, her breast still heaving with the queer, dry sobs. He looked at her for a moment and then left the room without another word and went downstairs. Jane crept down behind him, wondering in a confused, frightened fashion if she had dreamed the whole thing.

But Allison still lay in the drawing room, the pool of blood framing her blonde head, her blank eyes gazing at nothing.

John knelt down and looked at her, touching her wrist for a moment, and then straightened up and made for the phone. He called a doctor first, and the police, and after standing for a while, frowning at the floor, turned on Jane.

"Tell me what happened as quickly as you can."

"But I don't know," she protested. "I came down here and found her like that."

"Why did you come down?"

"I heard—" she hesitated, and her voice trailed off. He'd never believe that she'd heard the piano playing, and yet what else could she say? She looked at him with wide, scared eyes, and decided, at last, to tell the truth.

"It was the piano, John. I heard it playing last night and then again tonight. And don't tell me I imagined it, because I didn't."

He gave her an odd look and said flatly, "I haven't heard it."

"I know, but I'm directly above this room, and I think the sound carries through the hot-air register."

"What else did you hear?"

"Nothing," she said rather desperately. "Nothing at all but the piano."

He continued to question her until the arrival of the doctor and the police, when he abandoned her with a last warning look. She had no idea what the look meant.

It developed that Allison had been struck several killing blows on the back of the head. The local police chief, who was a big, slow-moving man, took it all very calmly, but his two assistants were excited almost to fever pitch. They both jumped when Dolly appeared unexpectedly and let out a shrill scream, but Chief Evinston merely said, "Switch it off, girl, and don't make a pest of yourself," so that Mamie, who had been going to scream herself, closed her mouth and gave Dolly a contemptuous look.

Chief Evinston seemed mainly concerned over the expected arrival of Allison's father. He kept peering out of the window for the sight of approaching headlights and managed only a few rather absent questions in between.

Why had Jane come downstairs? What had she heard to arouse her?

Jane began a stammering explanation and was cut off short by John. He said firmly, "My wife is in the habit of coming downstairs at all hours of the night. She is too thin and doesn't sleep very well, and the doctor advised her when she had a wakeful spell to get something to eat."

Chief Evinston said, "Oh," and after another searching look out of the window added, "What made her come into the parlor here?"

"She heard a noise," John said promptly. "Nothing that she could identify, but she came and looked in. The doors were closed, and that struck her as peculiar, since we don't usually leave them closed. She opened them and turned on the light, and of course saw the poor girl at once. She came straight upstairs and woke me."

Chief Evinston nodded and looked at Jane, who nodded back at him. John had suppressed the piano playing, and she supposed that he was right. It did sound absurd. Only why did he cover up for her when he had this chance to throw her to the wolves? Of course. He didn't want any scandal, as it would hurt his business. It was his own skin he was trying to save, not hers. And why should he save hers, anyway?

Allison's father arrived eventually, and there was a rather painful scene. He wept bitterly at first and then became fairly belligerent and swore revenge on his daughter's slayer. In the end, he demanded that Dick Rouston be produced forthwith.

Chief Evinston, who had patted him on the back futilely once or twice, asked whether Allison had had a date with Dick for that evening, but Mr. Ketria declared that he did not know, since Allison had rarely told him where she was going when she went out. The chief so far forgot himself at that point as to observe that his own daughter always told where she was going and when she went out, or stayed at home.

Mr. Ketria turned an inflamed eye on him, and Chief Evinston backed away hastily and asked for the telephone.

John displayed it, not without pride at having been able to get it installed so promptly, but Chief Evinston brushed that aside impatiently and asked if they knew the Rouston number offhand. Jane opened her mouth to give it, but John said quickly, "No, we don't. I'll look it up for you."

After he had found it, the chief nodded and waved them imperiously out of the hall. They returned to the drawing room and sat down close to where Mamie and Dolly, sworn enemies up to this time, were now more or less clinging together on the sofa. Allison still lay where they had found her, and Mr. Ketria sat beside her on the floor. He was weeping again.

Jane thought of Mrs. Ketria, a timid little mouse of a woman who had always been more or less kicked around by both her husband and Allison. Someone should telephone her, Jane thought uneasily. She was almost certainly sitting at home, waiting and wringing her hands. Mr. Ketria would never have brought her with him.

Jane stood up and went quietly toward the hall, but John was beside her instantly and stopped her at the door.

"Where are you going?"

"I want to phone Mrs. Ketria."

"Is there a Mrs. Ketria?" he asked, and made it plain that she was not supposed to know.

"I don't care," Jane said defiantly. "I'm going to phone her anyway. Her husband won't bother about her for hours yet, and she should be told. She may want to come over here."

Evinston appeared behind them, and Jane turned to him. "Someone should get in touch with Mrs. Ketria."

"I don't want her here," the chief said emphatically. "Tell her to go to the hospital. We're taking the body over there for a p.m."

He went into the drawing room, followed by John, and Jane lifted the telephone with clammy fingers. She was very nervous and did not know how to say what must be said. As it happened, Mrs. Ketria made it easy for her. She said at once dully, "She's dead, isn't she?"

"Yes. I'm sorry."

There was a silence, and then Jane asked anxiously, "Is there anyone with you, Mrs. Ketria?"

"Yes, my sister Midge is here. I don't need anything. But I want to see my daughter."

Jane told her to go to the hospital and presently put the phone down with a feeling of infinite relief. As she turned away, Dick came in the front door. He saw her but swung abruptly into the drawing room without a word or a sign of greeting to her. She sank onto a chair near the telephone, feeling sick and deadly tired, and hoped desperately that she would not have to look at Allison again.

Dick came out almost immediately. He walked straight over to her, and she knew at once, by his attitude, that he intended to make trouble. She stood up, her hand on the back of the chair to support herself, and saw that John was watching them from the doorway.

Dick came close to her and spoke venomously through gritted teeth.

"I should have had you put away before, you damned lunatic, but now I'll see that you hang."

CHAPTER 20

JANE STIFFENED and backed up against the wall. It was all over, then, and she'd have to take what was coming to her. She'd done wrong, and now she was going to pay for it. She tried to speak, but before she could get the words out, John was standing between them.

"What was that you said?" he asked Dick.

Dick gave him a contemptuous glance and turned back to Jane.

"Did you think I wouldn't know you? You've done a good job on yourself, all right, but you *were* my wife, and I'm not a complete fool."

"Then you know Jane," John said sharply.

Dick flung around toward him. "I suppose you're in on it, too, this filthy plan to kill off poor Allison!"

Jane looked at him and thought vaguely that he was genuinely badly upset. She was conscious of other people being in the hall, but it didn't seem to matter much.

John was saying, "Don't be absurd. And if you know Jane, tell us immediately. She is suffering from amnesia, and we are very anxious to find out who she really is."

Jane felt relief like a cool breeze through her entire body. John had found the one logical way out of this mess, and she'd stick to it. Surely this would settle everything. And she'd pay John back all the money she owed him.

She glanced at Dick and stiffened again immediately. He was smiling in a way she knew well. It meant that he was up to something.

He removed the smile, passed his hand over his head, and closed his eyes for a moment. "Please forgive me," he murmured. "I must have been out of my mind. Just because this terrible thing happened in your house, I had no right to accuse you people of anything. It was very remiss of me. Please forget about it."

He was running true to form, Jane thought. Now that he had had a moment to think, he realized that it was more important than anything else to keep the money.

He turned to walk away, but John stopped him. "I'd like you to explain some of the things you said. You made it pretty clear that you know Jane. You called her your wife. You must—"

"No, no," Dick interrupted, "I was out of my mind with grief. It's just that there is some similarity—the eyes—but it was just shock. Poor Allison!"

He walked away and disappeared into the drawing room, and John looked after him thoughtfully. He might or might not have believed the amnesia story, but it didn't matter much. That would be it, and he'd prove in an orderly manner that she was Gloria. It should be easy enough.

Chief Evinston, Mamie, and Dolly were all in the hall and had heard the amnesia story. They were all curious. The chief asked for an immediate explanation and, when John asked to have it kept confidential, ordered Mamie and Dolly to make themselves scarce, to their fury.

However, there was an interruption. The ambulance arrived and Allison's body was taken away. Mr. Ketria and Dick started a loud, angry discussion, Mr. Ketria accusing Dick of having killed his daughter, and Dick declaring furiously that Mr. Ketria had allowed the girl to run wild. In the end, they followed the ambulance together in Mr. Ketria's car.

The chief heaved a sigh of relief as their voices died away and proceeded to herd Jane and John into the drawing room, where he closed the doors. "Now, what's all this about amnesia?" he asked.

John explained it briefly. "My wife was suffering from amnesia when I first met her, but she told no one about it except myself. She can remember having been pushed over a bridge but nothing before that. And she has no idea of her identity. Naturally, we were very much interested when Mr. Rouston said something about her having been his wife. It does seem to fit in, you see, and of course we're very anxious to have the thing cleared up."

Chief Evinston turned and stared at Jane. "Don't seem possible," he muttered, after a moment. "I remember Mrs. Rouston. She was a homely girl, nothing like your wife, Mr. Cowrer. Anyways, Mrs. Rouston's body was found and identified."

John nodded. "But I understand that that identification was never quite positive, and I believe you know that, Chief Evinston."

The chief looked down at the toes of his shoes and decided that they were a bit worn. Better get a new pair—take the money first and just buy them. No use talking it over with the wife. She'd be able to think of at least six things they needed more urgently.

John nudged him. "Wasn't there a mole missing from that body?"

"Nah," said the chief irritably, tearing his eyes away from his shoes. "The body was too decomposed to tell. You couldn't have seen a mole if it hadda been there."

"If the body was that far decomposed, I don't see how there could have been a positive identification."

"Look, mister," the chief said pugnaciously, "the case of Mrs. Rouston is in the closed files, but this here murder is wide open. I got work to do, see! And my left foot looks more like Mrs. Rouston than your wife does."

"You won't object, however, if I investigate the possibility?" John asked imperturbably.

"You investigate," said the chief, "until your tongue hangs out, just so long as you keep outa my hair. Now, I'm going to question you folks."

He opened the door and admitted Mamie and Dolly, who came in with an air of having had their ears against it. When he had them seated, he began to question them with gusto. He wanted to know what Allison was doing in a house where she apparently had no business. He insisted that one of them should know why she was there and when she had come.

They all denied any such knowledge, and the chief, who had remained standing, shifted his weight from his good foot to the one with the corn on it. The corn protested sharply, and he shifted back again.

"Who let the girl in?" he demanded.

It seemed that no one had, and Mamie supplied brightly, "If any of us had let her in, we'd have known why she came, and when she came too."

Dolly backed up her enemy by saying virtuously, "That's right."

Chief Evinston gave them each a cold stare and asked, "Who locked up for the night?"

John remembered having locked the front door.

"Is that all?"

John nodded. "I figured Dolly would take care of the back door."

"What about the windows?"

John said that he had never given the windows a thought. That seemed to annoy Chief Evinston. He asked, "Do you mean to say you are not in the habit of locking the windows each night?"

John admitted that he was not, since it had never occurred to him. He explained that he had previously lived on the ninth floor of an apartment house, where you didn't have to think about locking the windows.

Evinston turned on Jane. "What about you, Mrs. Cowrer? Didn't you think of locking the windows?"

"It never occurred to me," Jane said vaguely, "to lock anything at all."

"Why not?" Evinston snapped. He was beginning to feel thoroughly exasperated.

"I don't know." Jane looked at him meekly. "I just never thought of it."

Evinston turned his attention to Dolly, who was distantly related to his wife. "What about you? Do you do any locking up around here at night?"

"I lock up the kitchen door, which is what I'm supposed to lock up," she told him aggressively. "The front door ain't none of my business except to let people in and out."

"All right, all right. What about the windows?"

"Same thing. I lock the kitchen windows, and that's all I lock."

Evinston looked at Mamie and said, almost persuasively, "What about you? I expect you locked the windows, didn't you?"

"You forget," said Mamie coldly, "that I am merely a guest here. Of course I did not lock any windows."

The chief would have been glad to knock all their heads together. If one of them had locked up the house, then he could concentrate on the four of them, because why would Allison come in at one of the windows and lock it behind her? But if she had been admitted through the front door, that was different. Actually, all the windows downstairs were locked, with the exception of one in the drawing room. He walked over moodily and examined it again. He moved the lock around and then saw that it was broken—a piece snapped right off. So they could not have locked it if they had wanted to.

He felt that they were getting restless behind him, and he hadn't finished with them yet. He wanted to find out what weapon was used on the girl's head.

As if echoing his thoughts, John's voice sounded at his elbow. "What was used to hit the girl?"

Evinston shook his head irritably and leaned down to examine the bottom of the window. Wilbur was supposed to have examined it thoroughly, but Wilbur had the brains of a louse.

It was a long window, extending right to the floor, and it opened out onto the side veranda. Evinston pulled it open a little way, and a draft of sharp, cold air blew in. Mamie shrilled a protest, but Evinston did not hear, for a piece of paper had flickered in and lay on the carpet at his feet. He closed the window and picked it up, turning it over curiously in his fingers. It was folded three times, and when he had carefully straightened it out, he read slowly, "Darling, meet me tonight. Same place."

CHAPTER 21

CHIEF EVINSTON closed his hand over the small square of paper and gave John, who had been peering over his shoulder, an irritated push.

John moved away, but he had managed to read the note. He supposed that Dick must have written it to Allison, but surely their meeting place could not have been in this house. Of course, Dick might not have written it at all. Allison was very attractive, and it might have come from another admirer, but even if it had, they would hardly be meeting here.

He glanced up to find the chief's eyes on him in obvious speculation. Did the man suppose that he had written that note to Allison? It was all right, though, because Allison had been away, and he himself had not been in town long enough to have had an earlier meeting with her. Certainly no one could prove that he knew her at all.

He looked Chief Evinston straight in the eye and said, "Look here, Mr. Rouston had the heat on in this place for several weeks before we moved in. The men were in here, papering and so on, and anyway, he wanted to give the furnace a tryout."

"So what?"

"So Allison and some man may have been using this house for a rendezvous, since it was warm and unoccupied. She wouldn't have known that we'd moved in, because she's been away, so that the writer of that note was able to get her here without any trouble."

Chief Evinston considered it, decided that it sounded pretty good, and gave John an evil look for having thought of it first. He closed his fist more tightly over the note and muttered, "Yeah. I'm gonna find the writer of that note." He glanced around the drawing room and decided to let them all go for the moment while he ran after Dick, because who else would address Allison as "darling"? John was able to follow this mental resolution, and he proceeded casually to burst the bubble.

"I don't see how it could have been Rouston," he observed to no one in particular.

"Why not?" the chief asked warily.

"He could have met her anywhere. After all, they were engaged to be married. There would be no object to their sneaking off here."

The chief was conscious of a slight feeling of shame, but he covered it up immediately by telling himself that that angle would have occurred to him shortly. These smart city lawyers were slick but not sure, not so sure as Chief Evinston, that is.

He told John curtly to sit down and proceeded to question the four of them. He went through all the routine questions that he could think of and made no headway at all.

Dolly was the only one who admitted to having been out, and she declared that she had come in around eleven. Unexpectedly, Mamie backed her up. She had heard Dolly come in, and it was around eleven.

Evinston fixed Dolly with a bloodshot eye and demanded, "Where'd you go at that time of night?"

"I had a couple sandwiches at Kelly's place. Any law against that?"

"Your own common sense ought to be against it," Evinston barked angrily. "It's no place for a woman alone at night, or any other time, either."

"Who said I was alone?"

"If you picked someone up in that joint it was worse than being alone," Evinston shouted. "Why don't you go out with a decent man to a decent place?"

Dolly, fiery red in the face, drew in her breath for a vituperative retort and was frustrated by Evinston, who took an unfair advantage of his position. He snapped her to silence and turned his attention to someone else.

Dolly subsided, fuming and muttering, and was not comforted by an expression on Mamie's face that seemed to say "I told you so." She was conscious of an impulse to remove the expression by violence but forced herself to inaction by grimly thinking of her new dress.

Chief Evinston, now thoroughly bored with all of them, suddenly ceased his questioning, and telling them all to remain in the vicinity where he could get at them when he wanted them, departed abruptly.

As a matter of fact, he was after Dick, because he could not rid himself of a feeling that Dick held the right answers.

John locked the front door after him and told the others to go up to bed. He added that he would attend to the locking up of the entire house.

"No, sir. Nothing doing," Mamie said vigorously. "Do you think I could go to my pillow and sleep sweetly after all this? I'm trembling like a leaf, and I'm going to have some strong, hot coffee."

Dolly nodded. "O.K. I'll make it." She headed for the kitchen, but Mamie caught up with her and they walked abreast, having a little difficulty at the doorways.

Jane followed as far as the dining room, where she dropped onto the seat in the bay window. There was a hot-air register close by, and the seat was fairly warm. She thought vaguely that if John had slept here last night, he could not have been too cold, after all.

She glanced up and saw that he was standing beside her.

"I thought of that amnesia business on the spur of the moment," he said in a low voice. "It seems to be a pretty good angle and ought to settle everything with little or no trouble. I think I can prove your position, and then you can go back to your own home."

Jane nodded, without words, and stared at the dining-room table. It was a nice table. She liked it. She liked all the furniture she had bought for this house, but it was not for her. She was to go back to that big, gloomy old house and wait to be killed. Probably the second effort would be more efficient.

She gave her head a little shake. No. She didn't have to live with them. She'd work it out some other way, somehow. She was lucky to get out of this mess so easily, and it was because John was helping her. It was good of him to help her, when she had done him such an injury, and done it with her eyes open.

She removed her absent gaze from the dining-room table and looked at John's dressing robe. It was a good robe, sober and conservative like John himself. He was honest and decent, not given to telling lies, so that when he did tell one, like this amnesia story, no one thought of disbelieving him.

She stood up, her hands fumbling nervously at her own robe. "I—I haven't really thanked you for what you did. You pulled me out of the mess I had got into very, very neatly. I'd appreciate it if you'd take steps to establish me back to myself again. And I can't tell you how sorry I am about all the harm I've done you."

John was lighting a cigarette, and he gave her an oblique glance. "Quite a speech." He turned away from her and added carelessly, "Listen to that pair chattering out in the kitchen. I'll bet it's you they're discussing, rather than poor Allison."

Jane, back on the window seat, hanging her head, made no reply. He intended to get rid of her as soon as possible, she thought. And why not?

John walked around and examined the furniture. A table, four chairs, and a low dresser.

"Four chairs," he said presently. "Weren't expecting much company, were you?"

She looked up and said slowly, "They're good chairs, and there is a bridge table with four matching chairs which would blend in with these very well, so that actually we could have seated eight people with more or less elegance."

He nodded and then was nearly pushed over as Mamie and Dolly burst in from the kitchen with a loaded tray. Dolly started to lower it to the table, but Jane sprang up and cried, "Wait, I'll put something down to protect the surface."

Dolly waited until a cloth had been spread over the table and then put the tray down with a thump. "That sure sounded like Miss Gloria, but I don't see how you can be her, Mrs. Cowrer. She was as homely as an old umbrella, poor lady. I'll show you a snapshot I got of her."

Mamie was distributing the cups, and she said sharply, "Don't be stupid, Dolly. Didn't I tell you she changed her looks completely? She must be that Gloria. Isn't it a mess?" She looked at Jane and John with a sudden cheerful smile. "You'll have to divorce that Dick, Jane, so you can marry John again."

"I'm afraid you don't quite understand, Mamie," John said quietly.. "I have no intention of taking another man's wife away from him. If Jane is Gloria Rouston, she must go back to her husband."

Dolly, who was still dawdling around the tray, forgot herself and said eagerly, "You got no need to worry about him, Mr. Cowrer. He don't want her. I know for a fact that even before she disappeared he went to see a lawyer to find out couldn't he divorce her."

CHAPTER 22

MAMIE AND JOHN each turned a cold eye on Dolly, and she muttered defensively, "I guess I open my big mouth too much." She started out of the room, but John called her back peremptorily.

She gave him a scared look, and he said flatly, "I want you to tell me a few things."

Dolly belted her old robe more tightly about her with nervous fingers and hovered uneasily by the swinging door that led to the kitchen. She watched John in silence while he seated himself in front of a cup of coffee, observing to no one in particular that he couldn't see why anyone wanted coffee at this time of the night.

He presently glanced at Dolly and said, "You say that Mr. Rouston had consulted a lawyer about a divorce?"

Dolly swallowed a mouthful of air and then nodded.

"When was this?"

"Last summer, Mr. Cowrer. Early summer. June, I think."

"What was the outcome?"

"Huh?" Dolly said confusedly.

"What happened? What did the lawyer say?"

"Oh." Dolly twisted her face and squinted in an effort at concentration. "Well, I'm not exactly sure just what he said, except he told him to go fly his kite."

"To—what?"

"Told him nothing doing," Dolly said, more simply.

"I see. And what made Mr. Rouston think he could get a divorce? As far as I can make out, his wife was dull but blameless."

Dolly nodded. "Yeah. Well, I guess that was why the guy told him no soap."

"Do you know on what grounds he wanted to base the divorce?"

"Er—yes. In—incontinence—incompetence, something like that."

"Incompatibility?"

"That's it! That's what it was!" She tried to insinuate herself through the swinging door at this point, but John called her back again.

"Do you know the name of the lawyer he consulted?"

"No, sir. He went to the city. He wanted one of those real slick fellas."

"And do you mean to tell me that the man wouldn't even try?"

"Wouldn't touch it," said Dolly. "I know for a fact."

"All right." John thought it over for a moment and then said, "Now tell me about something else. The family were thinking of having Mrs. Rouston examined by a doctor because they thought she was mentally unbalanced. Did you think so too?"

Dolly's eyes slid around to Jane, but she shook her head firmly. "No, sir, not me."

"Why did they think so?"

Dolly considered it before she said slowly, "Well, she hardly ever spoke, see, and then, when they spoke to her, half the time she didn't seem to hear."

Jane twisted clammy hands together and thought frantically that it was exactly what she had done, and what she was still doing.

John thought of it too. He glanced at her, found her eyes on his face, and looked away again quickly. .

"Is that all?" he asked Dolly. "They thought she was losing her mind because she was silent?"

"There was other things, too."

"What, for instance?"

"Well, for one thing," Dolly said thoughtfully, "she got up early in the morning and stuck her head out of the window, winter and summer, this was, with her head hanging down."

Jane started up from her chair, the color dark in her face, but before she could say anything, John spoke quickly and harshly.

"Be careful, Jane, you'll spill the coffee."

She sank back into her chair, shaking with the realization that she had nearly given herself away, and was silent as John turned back to Dolly.

"That's nonsense, Dolly," he said firmly. "How could they think a thing like that was a form of insanity? She probably had heard over the radio that it would beautify her neck or something of that sort. Everyone seems agreed that she was not very pretty, and here, where everyone knew her, she'd be ashamed to make any obvious changes. But as soon as she fell over that bridge and lost her memory, the first thing she did, you see, was to change her appearance entirely."

Dolly looked at Jane again and shook her head dubiously. "I just can't believe it. She don't look like Miss Gloria no more than I do. Anyways, about hanging her head out, she said she was trying to get some fresh air. But with the temperature at zero sometimes they thought it was kind of queer. It never bothered me none, though. I always believe in do in what you feel like, no matter how crazy."

John nodded, and suddenly dismissed her. He told her to go to bed and leave the coffee cups until the morning. She eased herself through the door, and when it had stopped swinging, laid her ear against it.

But there wasn't anything to hear. John got up almost immediately and said, "There's nothing more to do tonight. I'm going to bed."

He went out and could be heard making his way up the stairs.

Mamie poured herself another cup of coffee and shook her head. "The poor boy," she said with a long sigh. "My heart aches for him."

"Don't!" Jane said sharply. "Don't be foolish. What's the difference, anyway? He's all right. Most husbands would be glad of an easy way to get rid of their wives. Look at Dick, toiling into the city, trying to track down a divorce. I'll bet he's having nightmares at the idea of getting me back again. Apparently he knew who I am all the time and wouldn't say so. And now he's denying it."

"Well, but that's just fine," Mamie said cheerfully. "All you have to do is to divorce him and marry John again. You wouldn't have to fool around with that incompatibility, either. You could divorce him for getting engaged to another girl while your back was turned."

Jane laughed hysterically. "Come on, Mamie, we'd better go to bed. I'm so tired that I'm silly. And can't you see that John has gone a bit sour on me? After all, he didn't know that he was marrying a— a bigamist."

"Can't you remember anything?" Mamie asked, as they climbed the stairs.

"Well, I—it seems as though things here were getting more familiar. I should have gone to a doctor, of course, but I was embarrassed." Her voice trailed off, and she thought nervously that she should not talk so much. She'd be getting into trouble. It was much safer to keep quiet.

She slept lightly and restlessly for the rest of the night, with an uncomfortable feeling of being on the bed but not in it. She woke early and, knowing that she could not sleep again, dressed and went downstairs. Mamie was still sleeping, but John was there, and she had a rather silent breakfast with him. He was impersonal and cold, and Dolly, waiting on them with flapping ears, heard nothing of interest. She had retired to the kitchen in disappointment and was banging pans around, so that she did not hear John when he finally spoke.

"You'd better get your things packed," he said, looking down into the coffee he was stirring. "I'm going to work on this mess this morning. I want you to stay in, in case I need you. It shouldn't take long to establish your identity, and then you can return to your own home immediately."

He looked up at her and had a moment of acute discomfort. The dark violet eyes were so very expressive, and they were fastened on his face with a look of hopeless misery.

He departed rather hastily, and Jane watched him go, quite unconscious of the fact that there had been any expression whatever in her eyes. She was thinking of that other house, where she had been so unhappy and where she would be frightened now as well. No, she thought, I can't go back there. I'll have to go somewhere else.

She went upstairs and began to pack her things. Why stay in the town at all? Once her true identity was established, she'd get some money and go far away and never come back.

Mamie came into the room with a lavender-and-green wrapper billowing about her and cried, "For mercy's sake, Jane, do you have to rush out of here right away? I can't see where a few days would matter."

Jane snapped a suitcase shut and said quietly, "It's better this way."

A sound of footsteps on the stairs brought Mamie whirling around to face the door, her hands clutching at the flying wrapper as John appeared.

He said, "Hello, Mamie. Where's Jane?" And as he looked over her shoulder, "Oh, I see."

"Only she's really Gloria, isn't she?" Mamie said wonderingly.
John shook his head grimly. "That's just the trouble. She isn't."
Jane raised her head. "What?"

"The whole family," John told her, "is in a solid block. They swear
that you are not Gloria, and they swear with equal vigor that they saw
Gloria's body and buried it."

CHAPTER 23

JANE'S FIRST FEELING was one of relief. At least she would not
have to go back now to that terrible house. But it left her without
funds. She was absolutely penniless. She had no right to John's money,
and she could not get at her own.

John said, "Looks as though it might be a tough fight to establish
yourself, and I haven't the time to do it. Moreover, it is a job with
which I had better not be associated. You must get some other lawyer
to see you through. You're bound to win in the end. I think Rouston is
playing a losing game, particularly since he knows you and has practically admitted it. There are several people, including Chief Evinston,
who heard what he said to you in the hall last night. Of course he's
denying that now and declares that we were mistaken in our interpre-
tation of what we heard him say."

Mamie said rather dazedly, "But why are they doing it? What's
the object, I mean?"

"Money," Jane replied shortly. She looked at John. "Then I'll just
take my things and move in there. The place is mine, and they've no
right to try and keep me out."

"No, no," he said irritably, "you can't do that. Go and get a lawyer. You must have had one when you lived here before. Ask for his
advice and follow it."

Jane said nothing, and Mamie looked from one to the other of
them rather helplessly. John, after a moment's hesitation, turned on his
heel and left.

He had not said anything, Jane thought, about her staying on here
until the thing was settled. Well, she'd have to get out, go somewhere.
She roused herself and realized that she'd been pacing the room aim-

lessly. That was no good. She must pull herself together and do something definite. She had been asleep all these months, or out of her mind, or something, to have done such an awful thing. Bigamy. No, it was amnesia, and she'd stick to that, and she'd find out who pushed her over the bridge, too. But who killed Allison? Chief Evinston was in charge of that. It had nothing to do with her. She'd have to get a lawyer, though, but who? The one she'd had was also Dick's lawyer, and he'd always thought a great deal more of Dick than he had of her. It had better be someone out of town.

She plunged into her packing with almost frantic speed, and Mamie, sensing a dangerous mood, helped in silence. It was soon done, with bits of lace and ribbon sticking out at the sides of the suitcases.

"I don't know why you're in such a rush," Mamie said in a subdued voice. "We did that much too fast. All your things will be ruined."

"I want to get it over with," Jane replied briefly.

She called a taxi and had all her luggage piled into it. She had decided to go straight to the house, her house, and she found herself laughing a little. It would be funny to be thrown out of her own home.

The cab driver looked at her curiously. He frankly admitted to himself that he could not make head or tail of it. The big murder had happened at this place only last night, and here was the bride fleeing to a neighboring house, the home of a well known wolf. When they arrived at the Roustons' he was further puzzled to see Jane take a key from her bag and open the front door, after which she directed him to bring her luggage into the hall.

The ensuing noise brought Sally out from the living room, her delicate eyebrows raised in inquiry. She looked at Jane and the suitcases and exclaimed, "Good heavens! What's all this?"

Jane looked her straight in the eye. "Is anyone using my room, Sally?"

"Oh dear!" Sally cried agitatedly. "Dick told me you were making some preposterous claim to being my poor Gloria. How could you do such a thing? How could you!"

The taxi man, bringing in the last suitcase, let it drop on his foot, and at the same time Chief Evinston appeared from the direction of the living room. The three of them stood and looked silently at Jane.

Jane kept her eyes on Sally. "I know I look rather different, but I think you know me anyway. I can tell you anything about the past that you want to ask."

"You mean your memory is back?" Evinston barked.

Jane looked him over. "Yes, it's back." She saw the disbelief in his face and added, "It's been coming back in rather a rush."

He narrowed his eyes a little and observed flatly, "I think you're playing a losing game."

"Of course she is!" Sally cried shrilly. "It's dreadful! I suppose it's a wicked scheme to get my poor niece's money."

"You planning to stay here?" Evinston asked.

Jane nodded. "After all, it's my house."

Sally straightened her neck, pulled in her stomach, and inflated her chest. "Indeed," she said, in a *grande dame* manner. "It is not your house, nor are you going to stay here. Really! Such bold effrontery!"

Chief Evinston broke it up. "You dames can settle this later," he said, too hastily, because an instant later he knew that he should have called them ladies. "I'm going to take Mrs. Cowrer into the living room for questioning," he added, speaking loudly in an effort to cover up.

Sally was exasperated. She wanted both Jane and the chief out of the house, but of course it was a case of murder and it was foolish to antagonize the chief. She stepped aside and watched Jane intently as she walked into the living room. There was something about that walk, she thought uneasily, and the eyes. But surely it couldn't be. After all, Dick should know, and he had declared positively that the woman was not Gloria. He had said that he'd been fooled himself for a while, and he thought he'd been deliberately led on, but he'd come to the conclusion that these people were engaged in a fancy racket to defraud him of his late wife's money. On the other hand, though, that body had not looked much like Gloria.

Sally shivered and looked at the taxi driver for a full minute before she realized that she was looking at anything. She suddenly came back to her surroundings and asked crossly, "What do you want, Gus?"

"What do I want?" Gus said, aggrievedly. "In the first place I ain't been paid yet, and anyways, from what I heard, it seems like the lady is going to need me some more."

Sally rumpled her hair fretfully. "Of course she's going to need you. She can't stay here, and I'm not going to pay you, either."

Gus extracted a battered cigarette from his pocket and sat down. Sally frowned at him and suggested that he wait in the kitchen, but he said composedly, "Not me, lady. I consider myself good enough to sit in any part of the house."

Chief Evinston had figured cannily that Jane should be able to tell him something about Dick. Either she was Gloria and should know Dick intimately, or she was an impostor who would certainly have taken the trouble to find out all about him. Either way it ought to be duck soup.

Jane sat quietly in an armchair, facing him, her ankles crossed and her hands folded in her lap, looking, the chief thought, as though butter wouldn't melt in her mouth.

"You know, he said, and found that he had to struggle to keep the irritation out of his voice, "as I think I told you, Mr. Rouston admitted that this note certainly looked like his handwriting and that it was his notepaper, too. But he swears he hasn't written a note like that lately, not since last summer. Now, his wife was alive last summer, and he won't say who he was writing to then. Says it wouldn't be fair to the lady, but I figger if you're Mrs. Rouston you ought to know who it was."

Jane thought it over and said presently, "You really ought to ask Dolly."

Evinston made an impatient little movement with his hand. "Oh, sure, Dolly woulda known, but you can't trust her. Maybe she'd feel like telling me, and maybe she wouldn't. And maybe she'd name the wrong woman just to get even with somebody."

Jane nodded in silent agreement. The chief evidently knew Dolly well. She considered it for a while and then said slowly, "The trouble is that he seemed to be without a girlfriend of any sort last summer."

"Do you mean that he usually had a girlfriend, although he was married?" Evinston asked, trying not to sound shocked.

"Oh yes," Jane said easily. "He always told me that it didn't mean a thing, but he usually had a special girl. When he didn't, he was restless, and he was restless last summer. From May on, I think—very restless." She fell silent again, remembering, and Evinston watched her eagerly.

Presently she gave a little sigh and spoke again. "Yes, I remember thinking that he must have found a new one, just a week before I was pushed over that bridge."

CHAPTER 24

CHIEF EVINSTON felt a little baffled. He didn't see how this girl could be the Gloria who lay out in the cemetery under a fitting headstone. A fine headstone, as a matter of fact. George said they'd paid a fancy price for it, and George ought to know, because— The chief pulled himself back to the matter at hand with a thunderous clearing of his throat. This girl, now, how could he believe anything she said? But he could check up on Dick and try to find out if he did acquire a new girlfriend a week before his wife's disappearance.

He stood up. "Well, thank you, Mrs.—er—" He didn't know what to call her because he still had an open mind. Jane followed him out to the hall. He thanked Sally for her cooperation and was making for the front door when she stopped him.

"I've had Mrs. Cowrer's things put back into the taxi," she said firmly, "but I'd like you to stay until I am assured that she'll go quietly."

Jane looked at her and laughed a little. "Do you really not know me, Sally?"

"Please don't be absurd," said Sally, studying her thumbnail, which had a mother-of-pearl polish.

Chief Evinston rattled the change in his pocket and remarked, "If your story is true, I can't understand why you changed yourself like that. Why didn't you wait until you found your home and family so they could reckernize you?"

Jane shrugged it away carelessly. "I had my teeth attended to because they seemed to need it. As for my nose, I thought it had been injured in the fall, so I had it fixed as well. I had no way of knowing, then, that it had always been—well—"

"Some schnozzle," the chief supplied absentmindedly.

"The dimple is new, Jane went on, "but that was pure accident. My cheek was pierced when I fell."

"The fall didn't turn your hair red," Sally said tartly.

"I'm letting the natural color grow back. You'll see that it's the same as it used to be."

"It's not the same length," Sally observed, eying it coldly, "and to my mind that proves in itself that you are not Gloria. She never could be induced by any means whatever to cut her hair."

Jane nodded. "That was silly, all that hair piled up on my head. Anyway, when I had it cut and dyed, I had given up all hope of ever being recognized."

Chief Evinston laid his hand on the doorknob and said impatiently, "I think you'd better leave here, Mrs.—er—until we find out who the hell—er—who you are."

Jane turned her back on the hall and walked out of the front door without another word. It was cold outside, and she felt a sudden annoyance when she thought of the several good warm coats that belonged to her in this house and yet she was obliged to go around in the cheap, thin thing she was wearing.

The chief, in parting, asked where he could get in touch with her, and she told him, rather helplessly, that she did not know. The hotel, perhaps.

He drove off in his car, looking frustrated, and Jane stood by the open door of the taxi and watched Betsy and Pete Hoge coming up the driveway. As usual, she felt a stirring of anger at the sight of them. They looked at her curiously as they approached, and she said clearly, "Hello, Betsy. Pete."

Their faces went blank, and she said quickly "Now, don't tell me that you can't recognize me."

"Should we?" Pete asked, and Betsy giggled.

Jane kept her eyes on Pete's face. "Are you and Rose still on the verge of getting married?"

It was crude, and she knew it, but she'd always been like that, speaking too directly and making blunders. They ought to recognize that in her.

Pete shifted his weight and pulled out a cigarette. She knew that, she had startled him, but when he spoke, his voice was easy and careless.

"Were we ever?"

"Yes," said Jane, "you were. You know as well as I do that the two of you were to have been married as soon as you could settle yourself financially."

"Is that right?" Pete said amiably. He glanced down at Betsy and added, "Do you remember anything like that, sugar?"

Betsy gave him a lazy smile. "Of course. You had a crush on Mother for all the world to see."

"Crush!" Jane gave a chilly laugh. "It was a long-lasting crush. It went on for years."

The girl stiffened a little and said more formally, "Mother and Pete are old friends."

Jane looked at her. How could they, she thought despairingly, how could they allow the child to take this vain, shallow, irresponsible man seriously? But they had always been careless like that. They never troubled about anything except their own personal affairs. Anyway, it was quite clear that not one of them was going to recognize her. They had been well coached by Dick.

She gave them a brief goodbye and stepped into the taxi. She told the driver to go to the hotel and then leaned her head back against the seat and closed her eyes.

Gus glanced at her in his mirror and said chattily, "You coulda knocked me down with a feather, sayin' you was Mrs. Rouston."

"Do *you* think I am?" Jane asked.

Gus had an open mind and said so. He hadn't lived very long in the town and had not seen much of Gloria.

Jane closed her eyes again and felt a slight relaxing of her tension. She was relieved to be going to the hotel, because she hadn't really wanted to stay in that big, depressing house where Gloria had been so unhappy, and where Jane's life might perhaps be in danger.

When she arrived at the hotel she was told with courteous finality that they had no room for her. She even asked for and appealed to Bub, but although he was also courteous and very apologetic, he was quite firm. There was nothing.

She returned to Gus, who greeted her as an old friend. She explained that there was no vacancy in the hotel and asked if he knew of a furnished room, or something of that sort.

Gus removed his hat and scratched his head while his jaws dealt competently with a piece of gum. After a few moments of thought his eyes brightened and he nodded. "Sure, lady, I know a place. Hop in. The meals ain't so hot, maybe, and it sure does stink the place up when they have cabbage, but what the hell, it'll be a roof over your head."

Jane settled back into the seat again and found herself thinking of Dick. Who was it he had taken up with that week before she was pushed off the bridge? He had been telephoning someone. She'd heard him saying the same things that he'd said to her in the beginning and that he said to every new girl who interested him. During the course of these affairs he was always careful to tell her that they meant nothing. She hadn't cared anyway, this last time, but she had sensed a difference in Dick. He'd been more interested than usual in that one. The girl had not been staying near them anywhere when they were in the mountains, for Dick had made three so-called business trips that week, although he had been unemployed at the time.

"Cold, ain't it?" Gus observed sociably.

"Very." She let a moment pass and then asked, "Did you know that poor girl who was murdered last night?

"Yeah. Miss Ketria. Sure was tough luck. Don't you know who done it, lady? You was right there."

"Not when it was done," Jane said and shivered. She noticed that he had slowed his cab to a crawl, and she realized that he must have been waiting patiently for some time to talk about the murder. Well, perhaps he knew something that would help.

She hesitated and then asked, "How long was it after his—his wife went that Mr. Rouston and Miss Ketria became engaged?"

Gus forgot for the moment that this girl was claiming to be Mrs. Rouston, and he chuckled.

"I don't know for sure, but you can put your shirt on it that it wasn't long, because they was mushing around together before the poor dame was drowned."

CHAPTER 25

JANE FELT A LITTLE thrill, which she decided with some amusement must be a latent sleuthing instinct. She tried to sound casual as she asked Gus, "How do you know? I mean about Miss Ketria and Mr. Rouston?"

"Listen, lady," said Gus kindly, "in the hackin' business you get to know all kinds of things. That guy Rouston hired me once when his car was outa commission, and I took him and the dame out to a joint on the turnpike. The Red Rose. On the way out they was neckin' with their gloves on, but on the way back no holds was barred."

"When was this?" Jane asked.

"Couldn't give you no date," Gus said regretfully. "Last summer."

"Early or late summer?"

Gus shook his head. "Musta been some time in the middle—not early, not late."

Well, that was good enough, Jane thought. So it was Allison who had been the new girlfriend at that time, and Dick had been serious about it for a change. But with a girl like Allison he would have had to marry her or at least pretend that that was his intention.

It was simple, then. Dick had pushed her over the bridge to get rid of her so that he could marry Allison. Only who had killed Allison? Simple again. She had done it herself in a blind rage after she had found out that her husband had forgotten her so soon for another woman. She wondered, in sudden terror, how long it would take Chief Evinston to come to that conclusion. But he'd have to be satisfied that she was Mrs. Rouston first.

Gus drew up before a big, shabby, old-fashioned house on a side street and said, "Here you are, lady. We'll leave them bags where they are until you got the room, just in case."

Jane knew the place. It had been a boardinghouse for many years. She looked at it now and was engulfed by a wave of the blackest depression. She struggled against the feeling and reminded herself that she had no money. She'd even have to get a job so that she might be fed.

She forced herself to enter the place, and was out on the sidewalk again within the space of a very few minutes. In the first place, she had not enough money to pay a week's rent in advance, and secondly, when asked for her name, she had hesitated and then given it as Mrs. Rouston. This brought forth a peremptory demand for explanations, and when she had haltingly told what she could, she was promptly ushered out into the street.

She climbed back into the taxi, wondering why she was so honest. Why she could not simply have called herself Mrs. Smith? Gus shook his head sympathetically and said, "Well, lady, that was the only room in town I know about. You got any other ideas?"

"You'd better take me back to the Cowrer house," Jane decided. She added, "It's been a very nice ride. I've enjoyed it," and she gave a laugh which was touched with hysteria.

It was growing dark now, and she was tired and hungry, as she'd had very little to eat all day. She hoped John wouldn't be home when she got to the house. She wouldn't mind Mamie—it wouldn't be so embarrassing—but not John.

When she walked into the hall, he was standing just inside the drawing room. He turned and looked at her with his eyebrows raised a little, but he said nothing.

Jane began a self-conscious, mumbling explanation, but he stopped her and said abruptly, "I can't hear what you're saying."

"I couldn't get a room anywhere. I tried. I—may I stay here to-night? I'll try to get something tomorrow."

"Of course," he said impatiently. "Don't be ridiculous."

She felt ridiculous as she went out to tell Gus that he could bring in the luggage. When he had piled it neatly in the hall, she discovered that she had not enough money to pay him, and John had to do it.

"Next time," he said dryly, "find the room first and then move your things. It will be considerably cheaper."

She muttered, "Yes," and just stopped herself from adding, "sir." She felt the hysterical laugh rising in her throat again, and, gritting her teeth, she picked up two of the suitcases and stumbled up the stairs with them. Mamie did not appear, and it seemed probable that she was annoying Dolly in the kitchen. She decided to go to the kitchen herself and expose her chilled sensibilities to Mamie's warm personality.

She went into the bathroom, washed her face and hands, and then ran a comb through the cloud of soft red hair. Back in the bedroom, she saw that John had brought up her big suitcase, but she went downstairs without having unlocked it or even moved it.

In the kitchen, Mamie was showing Dolly how to mash potatoes. She gave Jane a friendly smile and said, "You shouldn't have gone in the first place. I told you not to. There's plenty of room here, and I think it's a crying shame for you and John to part, no matter what the reason."

"There's such a thing as living in sin," said Dolly austerely, her eyes on the mashed potatoes.

"Did someone tell you," Mamie asked furiously, "or did you find out for yourself?"

She drew Jane out of the kitchen, observing in an undertone that was yet audible to Dolly, "Quite impossible, isn't she? So crude."

John had disappeared, but Chief Evinston was in the hall, and he insisted on talking to Jane alone. They went into the drawing room, and Evinston asked, without any preliminaries, if Jane still contended that she was Mrs. Rouston. Jane, too tired to reply, merely nodded wearily, and Evinston frowned down at the carpet under his feet. If she really were Mrs. Rouston, he said, then things looked bad for her. Revenge on Miss Ketria—that angle.

Jane said she was sorry he saw it that way. She *was* Mrs. Rouston, and she had not murdered Allison.

The chief offered several veiled threats, until at last Jane stood up and faced him.

"Look here," she said quietly, "I can't find a room anywhere in town, and you have told me that I must stay around until this thing is solved. If you intend to arrest me some time, I suggest that you do it now and settle my problem."

Evinston gave her a look of pure outrage. "Oh, no, you don't," he said angrily. "No one is going to make a hotel out of my jail."

"What do you have to do to get in, then?" Jane asked flippantly. "Will you put me on the waiting list?"

John came quietly into the room, and Jane felt convinced that he had been listening outside the door.

He said, "She's a little upset, Chief. You mustn't be too impatient with her. Try to remember that she's not well."

"What's she walking around for, then?" Evinston demanded irritably. "She ought to be in bed."

"She's had a little difficulty about beds," John said in a bored voice. "There are not many available."

Jane began to move toward the door. "There's one upstairs, and if anyone wants to move me out of that, it will be necessary to carry me."

"Best thing you can do," John said. "Go straight to bed. You're exhausted." He escorted her to the foot of the stairs and urged her upward with a firm hand.

When she had gone, he went back to the drawing room and, lighting a cigarette, regarded Chief Evinston through a temporary haze of smoke. "All stuck up in a blind alley, aren't you?" he asked mildly.

The chief's face clearly agreed with this, but he said sourly, "Not at all. Things are clearing up rapidly."

John gave him an evil grin and took a turn or two about the room.

"I hope you're not making the mistake of suspecting Jane," he said presently.

Chief Evinston was still undecided as to whether he suspected her or not, so he assumed what he thought was a superior expression and remained silent.

"Because you're way off the beam," John continued, "if you are."

The way he felt was that he was way off the beam, period, the chief thought sulkily, and preserved his silence.

"She would never have lured the girl up here to her own home to kill her," John said. "Almost any other place would have been preferable, no matter where."

Evinston shifted the foot that had the corn on it, and said grimly, "Go on. I'm listening."

"Well, it seems obvious that someone went to considerable trouble to get Allison Ketria to this house."

"How do you mean?"

"The note," John said impatiently. "Apparently Allison and Dick used to meet here after the men had left their work and gone home. It was warm, and they had complete privacy. That note was probably written by Dick to arrange one of their meetings, and was used again last night by someone else, if Dick is in the clear. Allison could hardly have known that we'd moved in, but Dick did, and so did several other people. In any case, you may be sure of one thing. Whoever delivered that note to Allison, and so brought her up here last night, knew very definitely that Jane is Gloria Rouston."

CHAPTER 26

CHIEF EVINSTON extracted a toothpick from his pocket, and began absently to pick his teeth. It was a form of relaxation denied him at home, because his wife would not permit it.

"How do you figger that?" he asked finally.

"The murderer realized that Jane's identity as Gloria would be brought to light, and she would probably be accused of killing Allison in revenge."

"Clumsy," the chief commented.

"All right, but the thing's clumsy no matter how you look at it. Can you think of any other possible reason for luring Allison to this house and killing her here?"

"Unless it was your—er—wife. Convenient to do the job here."

"Jane is neither that stupid nor that lazy," John assured him. "You can take my word for it."

"You can't pin it on Rouston, then," Evinston said quickly. "Because he's denying that your wife is—er—his wife."

"Naturally, he must deny it. He knows it will come out anyway. You heard what he said when he first came in."

"Sure, I heard him. He accused your—er—his—the lady among other things, which he wouldn't do if he planned the whole thing. He lost his head because he was all roiled up. And he really was all roiled up, because I know the guy. He worked in my office once. I'm ruling him out."

John fell silent, his thoughts turned inward. He couldn't let them railroad Jane into this. He was quite certain that she was innocent of the murder. But Evinston was right when he said that Dick had been genuinely upset over Allison's death. He was convinced of that himself. Still, he was not sure that Dick could be ruled out entirely.

"I'm off now," the chief said abruptly. "Gotta get home to dinner. My wife is the impatient kind. But I want this Jane to stick around. If she tries to leave, I'll have every cop in the state out after her."

"You will?" John said mildly, with a faint smile on his face.

The chief ground his toothpick into two pieces. One of these slick lawyers who would want to know on just what charge he would have all the cops in the state out.

He turned to go, but John stopped him. "What motive do you intend to pin on Jane, if it turns out that she is not Mrs. Rouston after all?"

The chief stopped dead in his tracks and swung around. "What do you mean?"

"I believe you said yourself that she could not be Mrs. Rouston, that there was no point of resemblance between the two. The entire Rouston family have denied *en masse* that she could possibly be their Gloria, and so you have all convinced me too. She is not Gloria Rouston."

"Now, wait a minute—wait a minute," the chief protested. "I just got through questioning her and explaining that if she was Mrs. Rouston she was certainly under suspicion, and she stuck to it up and down and sideways that she was Gloria Rouston."

John, with the faint smile back on his face, carelessly examined his fingernails. "In the beginning, certain things seemed to indicate that she might be Gloria, so I told her to concentrate and try hard to remember. But although she's so anxious to know who she is, she really can't remember a thing. She just pretends that she can. Actually, it's more or less wishful thinking."

"Get her down here," Evinston said furiously. "I want to question her again."

"Oh no. She's ill, and she's going to stay in bed unless you can get a doctor to certify that she's well enough to come down."

The chief stamped his way out of the front door and slammed it behind him. Someday he was going to sit down and study all the fine points of the law. He was never quite sure whether these guys were bluffing or standing on their just rights. Doctor's certificate! When the girl was perfectly able to walk around on her two pins, with lipstick all over her mouth into the bargain. When this case was finished, he'd have to try and get a trip to Florida.

John went up the stairs to Jane's room. The door was half open, and the room in darkness, and he rapped on the panels, and then grinned at himself. Silly to be knocking on Jane's door. But the grin faded, and gloom crept up on him. She'd put him in a lousy position and had done it deliberately for her own ends. Why hadn't he simply allowed the chief to pick her up and pin this murder on her?

Jane called, "Yes?" and raising herself on one elbow switched the bedside light on. She lay on the bed, still fully dressed, and there was a small red crease on her flushed cheek where she had been lying on the embroidery of the bedspread.

"I've arranged with Chief Evinston, against his will, to have your identity switched back again," John said. "You are now Mrs. Cowrer once more, but we don't get on very well. Do you understand?"

"No," said Jane simply.

"Look. You're in an unfortunate position, and the best thing at the moment is to let the establishment of your identity drop for a while, at least until they find out who killed poor Allison. You're to stay here and declare that you can't remember anything. You'd better get into bed now, and I'll have your dinner sent up."

Jane nodded, wondering a little why she had to dine in bed, but she said nothing and decided to do as she was told since she did not want to cause John any more trouble.

He was turning away when she said haltingly, "Don't you think I'd better try and get a room somewhere tomorrow? I mean, I don't want to be a burden to you any longer."

"No," he said curtly. "Please do as I ask. I prefer to have it that way."

Jane nodded again, and John left. She got up then and started undressing. He had not told her why she was being sent to bed, and she wondered if it were just to keep her from the dinner table. The thought brought a blur of tears into her eyes, and she pulled herself up sharply. If she started crying over John, she'd never stop. Anyway, it was stupid to suppose that he just didn't want her at the dinner table.

If that had been his idea, he would have absented himself.

She propped two pillows behind her and put on a rather severely tailored little bed jacket which reflected Gloria's taste. She was glad now that she did not have to go downstairs. The bed was comfortable, and she was so tired, not so much physically tired, but there was a sort of mental weariness that seemed to drag at her body. Her head ached a little, and she decided, impatiently, that she was thinking too much. She picked up a book and began to read, determinedly. Her eyes slid over the words for several pages before she realized that she was thinking about something else all the time. She went back to the beginning and started again, and this time her mind picked up the thread of the narrative and was enough interested to stay with it. By the time Dolly came up with her tray, she was feeling much more relaxed.

"Here you are," Dolly said cheerfully. "Mister said you was sick, but he didn't tell me no more than that. Cute bed jacket you got on, only it's kinda plain, ain't it? I like them feathery things that fly all over, myself."

"Marabou."

"Yeah," said Dolly. "Anything you say. Listen, what is the matter with you? You look fine."

Jane laughed a little as she took the tray onto her lap. "I really don't know."

"Ah," said Dolly, "That's what I thought. You know what I bet it is?"

"What?"

"You're going to have a baby."

Jane, pouring coffee from a small pewter pot, was surprised to feel herself blushing. "I've denied that rumor before," she said placidly. "I now deny it again."

Dolly appeared to be disappointed. "Just the same you never know. I got a sister—Gert—and I don't know how many times she told me, 'Dolly, I'm sure I ain't pregnant.' And look at her."

"Seven," said Jane, "the last I heard."

"It's eight now," Dolly said gloomily.

Mamie's voice came sharply up the stairwell. "Dolly! What are you doing up there? We're waiting for our dessert."

Dolly fled, and Jane proceeded to eat her dinner. In fact, she ate all of it and returned to her book feeling vastly better and relieved entirely of the headache.

Mamie came in some time later, and they chatted amiably for a while before she departed with the tray. From the doorway she called over her shoulder that she intended to go straight to bed.

Jane picked up her book again, and although she was now actively interested in it, she presently went quietly off to sleep, still propped up by the pillows and with the light on.

It was the piano which eventually wakened her. She opened her eyes and lay perfectly still while the faint, eerie melody drifted against her ears. This ghostly intruder played all her own old pieces, and played them with her own touch.

She shivered and thought confusedly that she'd be willing to swear it was Gloria playing down there. The ghost of Gloria. And she was Jane Doe, Jane Doe Cowrer.

The music slipped into the "Moonlight Sonata," and she strained her ears anxiously. She had always loved it so, but there was one place where she had seemed possessed to make an error. It would be nice to hear it played properly. And it couldn't be Gloria's ghost if it didn't stumble over that bar.

A minute later she had broken out in a cold sweat, with the hair prickling along her scalp. The music halted and blundered at that difficult little place, and then went on again—exactly as Gloria had always played it.

CHAPTER 27

JANE GOT SLOWLY out of bed. She was frightened to the point of chattering teeth, but she felt that she must go downstairs. She must try to find out who was doing this thing. The music was still filtering softly into the room as she went out into the hall.

She wanted to wake John, or even Mamie, to give herself courage, but she resisted the urge and crept quietly down the stairs by herself. She could not hear the music now, and she had a scared, creeping feeling that perhaps it had been in her head. Only, of course, it hadn't. She must not let herself start thinking that way. The sound came up through the hot-air register.

The drawing-room doors were open, and the room lay before her, dark and silent. She advanced a few steps and turned on the light, and then looked fearfully at the floor. But there was nothing. The room looked ordinary and peaceful. No one was at the piano. No body lay on the floor. She crossed to the long window with the broken lock. There was no way of fastening it, but it was closed and did not appear to have been tampered with.

She turned suddenly and ran for the stairs, then realized that she had left the light on and had to force herself to go back and switch it off. She walked up the stairs after that, because running would be hysterical, and she was determined not to show hysteria. There was some reasonable explanation for that piano playing. There had to be.

She went back to bed and lay rigid for a long time, waiting for the music to start again. But there was no further sound, and toward morning she fell into an uneasy sleep.

Mamie brought her breakfast up at nine o'clock and woke her by rattling the shades up to the top of the windows.

"Gorgeous day. Might as well let the sunshine in." She helped Jane into the severe little bed jacket and appeared to feel about it as Dolly had done. "It's nice," said critically, "but I think there ought to be bows and frills on a bride's things. You could trim the neck with some little rosebuds and put a big satin bow in front."

Jane shuddered and took the breakfast tray onto her lap.

"My, but you're lucky," Mamie observed, sitting down on the bed and on Jane's feet. "When I was first married, I had to roll out at six o'clock, and no excuses. And the things that man wanted prepared for his breakfast! Thin as a rake he was too. I started putting on weight right away. In the end I had to sit and watch him eat that huge, delicious breakfast while I drank black coffee and ate dry toast. I had to do something. I was spreading like a bush."

Jane murmured in sympathy and looked at the loaded tray on her lap. If only she had the appetite to eat it all and enjoy it. But she'd eat as much as she could possibly manage. She could not afford to lose any weight, and she most certainly did not want to hurt Mamie's feelings.

Mamie continued to chatter, and although it was still early in the day she had all the latest gossip.

"It seems the Roustons' cook left last night, right after dinner, and they have nobody there."

"I thought," Jane said, sipping coffee, "that they kept two."

"Well, they did. They've been trying to get someone. You see, Dolly left them to come here, and they hadn't replaced her when the cook walked out. I hear they're driving into the city—left early this morning. That Dick is doing the driving, and Betsy and Sally and Rose all went along. Rose and Sally are going to one of those fancy employment agencies to look at prospects through their lorgnettes, I guess. Dick has some shopping to do, and Betsy is going to get some clothes. I suppose Rose and Sally will get clothes too."

"Dick will buy more clothes than any of them," Jane said, spearing a piece of bacon. "The girls just can't keep up with him."

"You don't say!" Mamie clicked her tongue. "You know I wonder Chief Evinston let them go. They might all just run away. Who knows who killed that poor girl?"

"They will never run away, leaving money behind," Jane assured her.

"Anyway, I understand they left the house in a terrible condition. Breakfast dishes all over the place, beds unmade, dust everywhere. No one has bothered to dust or sweep since Dolly left. The cook just didn't have time to do it, or that's what she said. And I guess that's right, too, because they have guests all the time. Dolly was telling me. Nobody ever told the cook whether there would be ten for dinner or no one at all. She'd just have to prepare something anyway, in case." Mamie thought it over during a period of tongue clicking, and added in a scandalized voice. "Such waste!"

Jane clicked in sympathy, and Mamie suddenly stood up and flitted toward the door. "Well, I have a lot to do, dear, and much as I enjoy it, I can't sit here listening to you all morning. Try and eat everything on your tray now. It will do you good."

Jane ate as much as she could and then pushed the tray away and lay back against her pillows with a cigarette.

She was thinking of the other house, her house, filled with dust, dirty dishes, and unmade beds. She'd always had the place spotless when she was there.

I'd like to see it, she thought suddenly. I'd like to see whether they have roses climbing up the walls there too.

Well, why not? The house was empty, and no one would know.

She got out of bed and began to dress quickly. She tried to keep her mind a blank so that her conscience would not interfere with her plan, and she presently went quietly down the stairs, pulling on her gloves.

Mamie walked into the hall as she had her hand on the knob of the front door.

"Jane! My dear! What are you doing? You're supposed to rest in bed today. You know you're not well."

Jane sighed and said resignedly, "I feel all right."

"But where are you going?" Mamie asked. She paused, and as Jane made no answer, she added with a little sparkle of anticipation, "Maybe I'll go with you. It's not so cold out, and even if you're walking all the way into town, I think I can stand it."

"I'm not going into town." Jane studied the doorknob under her hand for a moment and then decided to let Mamie come with her. What did it matter, anyway?

"I'm going over to—to my house. Since no one is there, I thought I'd have a look at it and see what they've done to the inside."

Mamie was arrayed in her coat and hat in something under half a minute. She was full of excited speculation and wondered, first, whether it was trespassing, only to suggest, an instant later, that it might be a good time to move in and hold the fort.

Jane laughed wryly. She had thought of it herself, but the idea was very distasteful, and then she remembered with relief that John had told her to stay where she was and hang onto the Jane Cowrer role.

She had an uneasy idea that John would not approve of this expedition, and she was nervously anxious that he should not be any more annoyed with her than he already was. But she could not resist going now, and Mamie would be very disappointed if she changed her mind.

They cut across the fields to a path that Jane remembered. Mamie stumbled now and then and asked breathlessly why they could not have gone by the road, but Jane insisted that it would save them walking boldly up to the house from the street.

Mamie was like a child on its way to the circus. When they approached a side door of the house, and Jane stopped to fumble with keys, she almost jumped up and down in her impatience to get inside.

"We could go around to the front door," she whispered breathlessly, "if you don't have the key to this one."

"Wait a minute," Jane said. "I'm pretty sure I have it. I don't want to go around to the front if I can help it. I'd rather not be seen. And, incidentally, please don't tell John about this."

"Of course not, if you don't want me to. But can't you hurry?"

Jane found the key, fitted it into the lock, and the door swung inward.

The kitchen was a confusion of unwashed dishes and pots, and as they wandered through the lower floor they found dust and untidiness. But Jane found a little secret pleasure in the fact that there had been no redecorating downstairs. The furniture had been rearranged, but there was nothing new, with the single exception of a large ornate cabinet. Jane gave it only a passing glance and decided that she did not like it.

They went upstairs, and there everything was very different. It had all been redecorated, and there was a blue room, a pink room, a yellow room, and so on. The ideas were much the same as had been carried out in the Cowrer house, and a lot of the old pieces had been replaced with new furniture. The decor was the latest, as pictured in the best magazines, and they walked soundlessly because the entire floor had been covered with all-over carpeting.

Mamie was a little awed. "Have we seen everything up here?" she whispered.

Jane shook her head. "Rose's room is back here. I'll show you."

The door to Rose's room was half open, and Jane walked in and then stopped dead.

Pete Hoge was there, busily rummaging through the bureau drawers.

CHAPTER 28

JANE BACKED quietly into the hall and held up a hand to prevent the peering Mamie from walking in. Their footsteps had made no sound on the heavy, expensive carpeting, and Mamie had been awed to comparative quiet by the elegance of the furnishings and fear of being caught, uninvited, in someone else's house. After one quick glimpse of Pete Hoge, she turned and fled.

Jane crept into Betsy's room. There was a connecting door between it and Rose's room, and since it stood partly open, she was able to get behind it and peer through the crack.

She gathered that Pete was looking for something small. He seemed to be going methodically through every inch of space in the drawers of the bureau, and the drawers were in a tumbled mess because that was the way Rose always kept them. She was never able to find her various belongings without rummaging and never bothered to tidy the confusion after she had found a thing.

Pete straightened suddenly, and Jane saw that he had a small box from which he proceeded to remove some ribbons, several keys, and three or four envelopes. She heard him give a low exclamation, and he picked out a small object, but although she strained her neck and eyes, she was unable to identify it. She thought there was a flash of light from the thing and decided that it was probably a piece of jewelry.

Pete dropped it into his pocket, replaced the contents of the box, and put everything back into the drawer. He closed it, looked carefully around the room, and suddenly departed, silently and quickly.

Jane remained where she was, motionless, for some time. The carpeting made it impossible to hear Pete's footsteps, and she had no idea where he was. After a while she heard him moving around in the lower hall, and her tension relaxed. But she was puzzled. What piece of jewelry could Rose be keeping in an old box filled with rubbish? It could hardly be valuable, since Rose had always been fearful of having her jewelry stolen and usually wore it all for safekeeping. The pieces that she did not want displayed on a particular costume she pinned inside her dress. Then, if this object were not valuable, why was Pete stealing it?

She smiled a little to herself. It was a clear indication of her opinion of Pete that she automatically labeled his act as theft. Had it been someone she respected, she would just as quickly have found some reasonable explanation of what she had seen. But it seemed natural that Pete was picking up something to sell that would bring him a little ready cash. Not much, though, for the thing could not have been very valuable.

She walked through into Rose's room and looked around. The decoration had gone wild here, but everything looked a little soiled and tarnished. It was hard to keep this sort of stuff clean, of course.

She went to the window and saw Pete hurrying down the driveway, making off with his loot, she thought, and smiled again. As he passed out of sight on the road, a figure stepped out from behind a bush, and she saw that it was Mamie. Mamie sent a quick look after Pete and came toward the house. Jane went downstairs to let her in.

She was blowing on her cold fingertips and laughing guiltily, like a child. "My dear, I never ran so fast in my life, but he didn't see me. I thought you'd get caught, for sure."

"Caught?" Jane said coolly. "There is no question of my getting caught here. This is my house. And I think most of them know it too."

"Maybe they know it," Mamie said wisely, "but they're not going to admit it. Anyway, you're not supposed to be that Gloria now. For reasons."

Jane shrugged and asked, "Which way did Pete go?"

"He seemed to be making tracks for the village."

Jane nodded and after a moment's thought decided to follow him. She was convinced that he'd go straight to the pawnshop. She'd have to hurry. He had a good start and had been walking rapidly.

Mamie was disappointed and said so with gusto. She wanted to see more of the house. There were many things she wanted to snoop into, and when would they get such an opportunity again? But she followed Jane into the village, complaining of the distance, the pace, and the way her feet were hurting.

They caught up with Pete on the outskirts of the town, and Jane slowed down. He passed the pawnshop and a jewelry shop which Rose and Sally occasionally patronized, and turned at last into the little shop where an old jeweler had sold dusty, old-fashioned things ever since Jane could remember.

She paused at the show window as though for a casual survey of the clocks and rings displayed there and could see Pete quite clearly as he stood at the counter. He pulled the small object from his pocket, and Jane had an uncomfortable feeling that she should go in and stop this illicit sale of Rose's property. But as she continued to watch, it began to seem doubtful, after all, that he was selling anything. The old jeweler had pulled a tray from under the glass counter, and Pete, with the small object still in his fingers, was studying the contents of the tray.

"What is it?" Jane muttered, completely puzzled.

"I can't stand it," Mamie said, settling her hat. "I'm going in and see."

She walked into the shop before Jane could say a word to stop her and gave both Pete and the jeweler a cheery good morning. Pete stepped back, and Mamie removed her wristwatch and handed it to the old man. "It goes too fast or too slow, depending on its mood."

The old man gave it one contemptuous glance. "Those little watches never keep time. How can they, with their guts all jammed together in a silly little case like that? I don't like to work on the things, and you ought to be satisfied if it goes at all. It's never going to keep good time."

Mamie's eyes had strayed to the case which still stood on the counter. It held ring settings, and a ring with what appeared to be a large diamond lay on a piece of velvet beside the case.

"When will it be ready?" she asked absently.

"When will what be ready?" the old man snapped impatiently.

Mamie realized that her watch had been refused. She drew herself up and announced haughtily, "I shall take it elsewhere."

"Good place for it," said the old man coldly. "Good day, madam."

Mamie turned her back on him and smiled at Pete. "Have a cup of coffee with us," she said cordially. "Jane and I are just going to drop in at the Forget-Me-Not."

Pete gave her a feeble smile, and the old man said pertly, "Many thanks, but I have no one to leave in the shop."

Mamie left without further words and with a strong feeling that she had been badly worsted. She joined Jane, and the two of them moved off together. Pete, watching them go, reflected that he might as well take Mamie up on her invitation and see for himself whether the red-haired dish could possibly be that gawk, Gloria. On the face of it, it seemed impossible, but you never could be too sure about anything.

He completed his business with the jeweler and made his way to the Forget-Me-Not.

Mamie had told Jane of the ring and the tray of ring settings, and Jane was more confused than ever. She could not remember Rose having owned a large solitaire diamond ring.

Pete came in and joined them with a charming smile. He looked at Jane and asked impudently, "Who are you this morning?"

Jane smiled. "Today I am Mrs. Cowrer."

"Ah, yes, silly of me not to have noticed. And what is Mrs. Cowrer's first name?"

"Jane," Mamie said rather tartly. It seemed to her that he was being just a bit too fresh.

Pete chatted on idly, but Jane's mind had drifted away into something else. That new piece of furniture in the Rouston living room, the ornate cabinet which she had not liked, was a radio-phonograph combination, of course, a new and expensive one. There had been an old one in that spot, she remembered, a machine with a recording device, and they had made their own records. She had made quite a number herself, recordings of her piano pieces.

And that was it, of course, she thought, wondering at the simplicity of the thing that had frightened her so much. The ghost of Gloria at the black piano merely meant that someone was playing those records in the middle of the night.

CHAPTER 29

"I'D GIVE A LOT to know what you're thinking about," Pete said, smiling at Jane.

She glanced at him and retorted rather absently, "Not for sale."

Mamie laughed heartily and then said to Pete, "That was a lovely ring you had in the jeweler's there. What lucky lady is going to get it?"

"Ring?" Pete said blankly. "Me?"

Mamie nodded. "I don't see why you're having it reset, though. I think it has a lovely setting right now."

"Oh." Pete stirred his coffee, and a faint color came into his face. "That ring wasn't mine. The old boy was trying to sell it to me. I told him I didn't like the setting, so he tried to back me into a corner by offering to reset it. I didn't buy it, though—I—er—"

"Who were you buying it for?" Mamie asked.

"Who said I was buying a ring?" He turned pointedly away from Mamie and said to Jane, "Did Evinston get anywhere in his investigation of poor Allison's murder?"

"He doesn't confide in me."

Pete shook his head and assumed, for a moment, a mournful expression. "Poor Dick's been hit hard."

"Did he love her so much?" Mamie asked sentimentally.

"Oh, sure. He was really sunk this time. Nuts about her."

"But he's seen her around for years," Jane murmured, speaking half to herself. "He never paid any attention to her before."

Pete grinned. "She only just grew up."

Jane thought about it and realized that it was true. Allison had been just a kid before last summer, and suddenly in the spring she had blossomed into a young lady, the most glamorous young lady the town had seen for some time. But why had she come to the Cowrer house that night? There must have been some reason.

Jane stood up abruptly and said to Mamie, "Pay my check, will you? I've just remembered a rather important appointment, and I'm a little late. Nice to have seen you, Pete."

"Wait a minute. Hey, wait!" Mamie said shrilly. 'Where are you going?

"Meet you in the hotel lobby in an hour," Jane called over her shoulder and hurried out of the place.

She was going up to the Ketria house to see whether Allison's Aunt Midge was at home. She was going to do what she had gone through so much trouble for—find out who had tried to murder her. It seemed very probable that the same person had killed Allison. And it must be stopped before there was some further tragedy. What had they in common, Allison and herself, that they had both been so murderously attacked?

Well, Dick, presumably. She had been Dick's wife, and Allison his fiancée. Perhaps it was some woman who wanted Dick for herself, so she killed off the competition. Only, that was silly. The woman would have to be deranged. She could hardly count on securing Dick for herself simply by killing off anyone who had a sentimental claim on him.

Chief Evinston's car stood in front of the Ketria house, but Jane gave it barely a glance. She kept outside the high hedge that surrounded the place until she reached the yard in the rear, where she scrambled through and went to the back door. She opened it without knocking and walked in.

Midge was there, sitting in a rocker shelling peas, and Jane drew a quick breath of relief. The woman's eyes were red and swollen from weeping, and Jane remembered, with a spasm of pity, that she had always been very fond of Allison.

Midge looked up in a startled fashion and clutched at the pan of peas.

"Please forgive me," Jane said hastily, "but I'm so very cold. I thought perhaps you wouldn't mind if I came in and warmed up."

Midge had always been a cordial soul, and she said, "Why, no, I'm sure you're welcome to come in and get warm. You do look half frozen. But who are you, my dear? I don't seem to know you."

"Well, that—no one seems to know, exactly. Who I am, I mean. I may be a newcomer here, and then again, I may have been living here for years."

Midge put the peas carefully on the table, and her eyes lit up. She had lived on gossip for as far back as Jane could remember, and it was the greatest pleasure she had.

Jane told her the whole story, sticking carefully to the amnesia version throughout, and Midge was enthralled. It was the most exciting thing by far since Dolly's black-haired sister Gert and her black-haired husband had produced a red-haired baby that looked more like the milkman every day of its life.

In the end, Midge looked Jane over very carefully, so that she could come to her own considered opinion as to whether Jane was or was not Gloria.

"I'd say not," she finally decided. "Really, you're nothing like poor Gloria. You're very attractive, my dear."

"Oh well," Jane smiled at her, "I suppose we'll find out someday."

"I should hope so, indeed. But you'll see that you're not Gloria, I promise you."

Jane nodded, and asked after a moment, "Has Chief Evinston made an arrest yet for poor Allison's murder?"

Midge's eyes filled with slow tears, and she shook her head. "No. He says he's going to arrest someone before the day is out, but I've heard that sort of story before."

Jane wondered for an uneasy moment if she were the fish in Evinston's net. But he had no real evidence against her, after all, especially since she was now Jane and not Gloria.

"How long had Allison been going around with Dick Rouston?" she asked Midge.

"Just as soon as his wife died." Midge compressed her lips for a moment, and gave her head a bothered shake. "It was scandalous. Her mother and I tried to stop it, but she was always very willful, poor child. And then, her father did nothing to discourage her. Of course he and Dick played golf and poker together, all that sort of thing. It was all very upsetting."

Jane moved restlessly about the kitchen, and when a pot on the stove began to bubble viciously, she automatically leaned down and turned the gas low under it. Midge, watching her, wondered why the action suddenly reminded her of Gloria and then decided that she was merely being influenced by the story she'd just heard.

"I suppose Allison was very much in love with Dick?" Jane said presently.

"Why, I suppose so, but you know how Allison was, with so many boys after her. Dick was crazy about her, and I guess she thought it would be nice to live in that house with all the money Dick had after his wife died. Money was always important to Allison, and then of course he was good-looking and she enjoyed going out with him. He was so much more sophisticated than the other kids who chased after her."

Jane nodded. Allison had not been in love with Dick, then, if Midge knew what she was talking about, and she usually did.

"You and your husband are living up at the old house, aren't you?" Midge asked. "I heard they had it fixed up. That old fool Evinston says Allison was in the habit of meeting Dick there, and this last time she didn't know you folks had already moved in. I told him he never made a bigger mistake in his life. Allison would never have met a man in an empty house like that. She was too smart. She always said she'd never let a man get the better of her, and she never did. If anyone got a date with Allison, he had to spend money on her. She saw to that. Her father always encouraged her, too. He said the men would have more respect for her if she expected the best. I always thought she carried it a bit too far. Sometimes it seemed mean. I remember one boy— But anyway, that's all over now. She was so pretty that she could get away with anything."

"I can't understand why she came to our house that night," Jane said soberly. "It must have been very late when she got there, and she didn't ring the bell, or we'd certainly have heard it."

Midge smiled for the first time. "Evinston says that she did. Insists on it, and he declares she didn't know you people had moved in. I knew all the time that the only reason she went there was because she knew you were there, but I was darned if I would tell him, the old fool."

Jane stared at her. "Why, what do you mean?"

"The poor child told me. She said, 'Auntie Midge, I've been finding things out all day long, and now tonight I'm going up to see this Mrs. Cowrer and tell her she'll have to give her husband to me, and not a peep out of her—or else.' "

CHAPTER 30

JANE WAS VERY still for a moment. She stood by the stove, looking down at the simmering pot without really seeing it. So Allison had known about her too.

Midge showed signs of faint embarrassment. "I don't think she was actually after your nice husband, my dear," she said uncomfortably. "You know how Allison was, maybe a little flighty. I thought she had seen him around town somewhere and thought he was attractive, and I supposed she was just fooling about going to see you. She was always saying some man or other was a dream. But you could have knocked me over with a feather when I heard she really did go to your house."

Jane realized that Midge was, naturally enough, a bit confused over the two husbands. She was under the impression that Allison had been referring to John, while Jane knew perfectly well that the girl had had Dick in mind.

"I suppose it was a bit of a shock to you," she said carefully. "After all, Allison was engaged to Dick, and it seems odd that she would come fooling around after a married man."

Midge nodded rather mournfully. "But, then, the child was so full of fun and high spirits. If she liked a man, she always told him so."

Midge began to cry, and Jane, after a few awkward words of comfort and condolence, slipped quietly out of the back door. No use in pursuing it any further, she thought. The subject seemed to have been squeezed pretty dry.

At any rate, Allison had known who she was. Dick must have told her. Probably he had phoned to wherever she was staying, and she had come back at once. But why had she come up to the house late at night and without an appointment? It was puzzling, but there must have been a reason and it would have to be uncovered.

She decided to return to the Rouston house and search Dick's room before she went home. He had always been careless with his papers and correspondence, and perhaps she would find something revealing. At least it was worth trying.

She began to hurry. She had to pass the hotel on her way through town, and as she came abreast of the entrance, she was hailed loudly from the steps.

"For heavens sake," Mamie called, "I thought you were never coming. You said an hour and it's been much longer than that."

Jane gave her watch a guilty glance. She had no idea whether it had been an hour, or two, since she had completely forgotten Mamie and the arrangement to meet at the hotel.

She did know, however, that Mamie's watch was not reliable, so she said firmly, "It has been just exactly an hour."

"I don't believe it," Mamie replied amiably, "but anyhow, let's have lunch. I'm starving."

Jane hesitated. She had practically no money, and it seemed silly to spend her few remaining pennies in Bub's hotel when Dolly could supply her free at home.

"Come on," Mamie said impatiently. "My treat."

"No, no—of course not," Jane protested.

"Are you refusing to break my bread?" Mamie asked. "What makes you so proud, anyway? When I invite my hostess to lunch, I expect her to accept graciously. Come on, will you, or I'll collapse from acute malnutrition."

They went inside to a table in the dining room, and Jane found herself embarrassed and even blushing when John appeared and was promptly hailed vociferously by Mamie.

"Oh, Mamie, don't," Jane muttered. "He probably wants to lunch with his business friends."

"Business friends, my eye," said Mamie. "He can eat with those bores any day in the week. You hear that, John?" she added as he approached. "Jane thinks you'd rather eat with those dusty old lawyers than with a couple of bright girls like us."

Jane's head receded into the collar of her coat, and she studied her fingers with the utmost concentration as John seated himself at their table. He said merely, "Anything decent on the menu?"

"I'm afraid to look," Mamie told him cheerfully. "I want a lobster, and I bet there'll be a choice between chicken croquettes and pot roast."

The Cowrers ordered quietly and briefly, while Mamie gave the waiter the set of instructions that were apt to accompany her orders. The waiter intoned the usual empty promises that her wishes would be carried out with infinite care, then departed, carefree and unburdened with remembrance.

John pushed the menu aside and looked at Jane. "You really should be at home in bed."

Jane raised her head, and her eyes widened a little. "Why?"

"Because Evinston will be suspicious of such a quick recovery."

"Was she sick?" Mamie asked.

"Certainly. She was so ill last night that Evinston was not allowed to see her."

"Imagine that," Mamie said wonderingly. "I thought it was just a little headache or something. Her head being weak, anyway, with all that amnesia."

"You'd better go straight home as soon as you have had your

lunch," John advised, "and we can only hope that Evinston won't catch you first."

"What could he do to me?"

"Well." John abstractedly straightened his cutlery so that it lay in precise lines. "Now that we have agreed with him in identifying you as Jane, he immediately suspects you of being Gloria."

"He's a bag of wind," Mamie said comfortably.

"I don't see why he should suspect me of harming Allison, even if I am Gloria," Jane protested.

"The jealousy motive gives him something to put his teeth into," John said with a touch of impatience. "I want you to go home and go to your room too. I don't want to see you put through the mill for no good reason."

"The best place for him to put his teeth," Mamie muttered, "especially at night, is in a glass of water."

A feeling of depression settled over Jane like a pall, but there was a glimmer of pleasure in the fact that John did not believe she had had any hand in Allison's death. She ate mechanically and had little to say throughout the meal.

Bub came to their table once and asked with a certain amount of manner if everything were all right. He was tingling with curiosity and tried to get them to talk, but even Mamie was brief with him, and he presently took himself off.

John paid the check, although Mamie protested a little, and then said curtly, "Go back home, Jane, and save trouble all around."

She said, "Yes," in a subdued voice, and Mamie exclaimed, "Oh, for heaven's sake, John, don't be such a fuss-pot!" .

When John had left, Jane said, "I'd better go home, Mamie, but you go ahead with whatever you want to do in town."

"But I haven't a thing in the world to do in town," Mamie declared. "I'll come right along home with you."

Jane still wanted to search through Dick's things before she returned to her room where, presumably, she was to stay, and she did not want Mamie with her. After a moment's thought she said casually, "All right, but I'm going to walk, you know. I feel the need of some fresh air. I expect you could find a lift from someone if you looked around."

"Oh, lord, Jane!" Mamie wailed. "My feet are raw right now. Why can't we just take a taxi?"

"Please, Mamie. I can't go home and just stay in my room unless I get some air first."

"You've been getting air all morning, hot and cold," Mamie grumbled. "Well, go on if you must, but I'll have to find something with wheels. If I tried to do that walk again, I'd fall flat on my face,"

Jane went off by herself and headed straight for the Rouston house. It appeared to be still deserted, and she felt fairly confident that the family would not return before evening, perhaps not until late at night. She knew them when they were on a spree in the city.

She let herself in at the side door and made straight for Dick's room. The house was quite silent, and upstairs her own footsteps were muffled by the carpeting. She began to go through his bureau drawers as quickly as possible but was slowed up a little because they were in the usual mess.

In the end she found two letters from Allison, but they were written in a sort of square script that looked pretty but was not very legible, so that she put them in her purse for a later reading. She was not troubled about Dick missing them. Her knowledge of him assured her that he would not be able to remember whether he had lost them or thrown them away.

She closed her purse and took a step toward the door and then stopped dead, frozen in her tracks. The door was swinging slowly inward.

CHAPTER 31

JANE HAD A SUDDEN feeling of utter absurdity as she stood with her heart thudding and her eyes fastened on the slowly moving door. She was in her own house and had every right to be there, and yet she was terrified.

There was no time to hide and no corner that would have hidden her very effectively anyway. She braced herself, with her head held high, waiting, and then, quite quietly, the door was closed again, without her having seen who was behind it.

For a while she continued to stand there, straining her ears, but there was no sound of footsteps on the thick carpeting, and she presently rallied her courage sufficiently to cross the room and open the door. There was no one in sight, but she could hear footsteps in the lower hall now, quick and light—a woman's steps.

Jane crept to the head of the stairs and was just in time to see Dolly disappear into the dining room. It was the sort of thing Dolly would do, Jane thought, and felt the fear drain out of her. Dolly loved snooping, and she knew that the family was away. There might be something more to it than mere idle curiosity, of course. Dolly was not exactly the trustworthy type, and there was so much going on that was mysterious that she could easily be mixed up in it in some way.

Jane went down the stairs and through the dining room to the side door. Dolly must have hurried, for she was almost out of sight across the fields by this time. How had she managed to get in? She had worked here, of course, and probably still had a key. That was simple enough, but what had she wanted in Dick's room? She must have been after something. She had always been sly and seemed to know everyone's business. Jane shook her head in perplexity and decided to postpone the problem.

She went back to the living room and examined the new cabinet, which was a combined radio and phonograph. There was a case for record albums and a great pile of loose records lying on the floor beside it. She looked through some of them but did not find any of her own recordings. It seemed probable that they'd have thrown them out if they had found them. In any case, someone had collected the things and was playing them at night where she could hear them. Was it an effort to drive her insane? And if so, why was it so necessary to get her out of the way? Well, she'd been a nuisance to them. Weren't they denying her identity when Dick, at least, knew perfectly well that she was Gloria?

She went back upstairs and sought her old room. It had been completely redecorated, and all her own things were gone. She'd had a small portable phonograph bound in dark blue leather for which she searched carefully, but it was not in the room. It was a guest room now, carefully correct and quite impersonal.

She went up to the attic and after a brief search found her own old furniture piled carelessly in a corner. The pieces were good, she thought, looking at the dust that had collected on them. Definitely Victorian, but good, and not hideous Victorian, either. She had grown up with that furniture, and she had always liked it. She was glad they had not thrown it away.

She could not find the phonograph, although she searched carefully. She returned to the second floor and looked hastily through the other bedrooms, but there was no sign of it. She was convinced that it was being used to play her records at night in order to frighten her, and if she could only find out who was in possession of it, it would at least be a start.

She returned to Dick's room and went through his personal belongings again. Dolly had wanted something in this room, and something Dick had acquired recently, since Dolly must have had free access in former times during the course of her housecleaning duties. She found nothing, however, and it was only when she picked up her purse in preparation for her departure that she remembered the letters from Allison which she had stuffed into it.

She was promptly convinced that they were what Dolly had been after, and Dolly was too late. She had them herself, and she was going to take them home and read them.

There was nothing more here, she decided. She might as well go home now. She went downstairs, out the side door, and started across the fields.

Dolly, she mused, must have seen her in Dick's room. She'd better have it out with the girl. Something might come to light. She thought of Pete and wondered whether he were going to try to marry Betsy. It was an unpleasant thought, and she frowned and quickened her steps. Betsy was only a child. It looked very much as though Pete had stolen the engagement ring from the girl's own mother. Certainly she did not actually know that, but she'd have to watch, and if Betsy displayed a new ring on her finger she'd act at once.

It was getting colder, and she pulled her thin, inadequate coat more tightly around her. Why on earth, she wondered, would Pete Hoge want to marry Betsy when the child had no money, not one penny? And he was old enough to be her father. Surely Rose would never allow it. She herself had given out a hint about the affair, but it was very evident that Rose didn't take it seriously. It was also obvious that she was indifferent about Pete's dereliction, although they had been good companions for so long.

It was odd that they had never married. They'd had no money, of course, but people of their sort were not given to letting a thing like that stand in the way of what they wanted. Someone had always been around to offer them a living.

Perhaps that was it, though. Rose might have figured that she'd have to go and live somewhere with Pete and take Betsy with her, and none of them would have enough money. So she might have decided to postpone her marriage with Pete until something turned up.

On the other hand, something had turned up. Her brother now had control over a considerable amount of money, and she could be assured of a comfortable living no matter what she did. And what did she do? She allowed Pete to wander off and attach himself to Betsy. There was something wrong about it, because Rose had a much stronger personality than Pete, and it seemed very unlikely that he'd have drifted away unless Rose had cut him loose.

Could she have told him to go and pick up Betsy? It seemed highly improbable. For all her faults, Rose was very fond of the girl, and had watched to see that no harm came to her.

Jane sighed and tried to drop the thing from her mind. She had entered the back yard of the house and could hear Dolly banging around in the kitchen, pretending, no doubt, that she had been there all day. She went into the kitchen, and Dolly gave her a warm welcome and inquired as to how she had arrived, as there had been no sound of a car. Jane glanced at her and decided that there was no use in asking her what she had been doing over at the other house. It would simply bring forth a torrent of voluble denials. Instead, she explained briefly that she had walked home and went to the stove to put on some coffee for herself.

"Let me fix that for you," Dolly suggested, working furiously on a bunch of carrots.

"I can manage, thanks." Jane went to the cupboard for a cup and saucer and asked after a moment, "Have you any idea why Miss Ketria came to this house so late at night?"

"Why, sure," Dolly said in some surprise. "I thought you knew.

She used to meet Mr. Rouston here, and then, that last time she didn't know you folks had moved in, and she got this note from the murderer, I guess."

Jane, manipulating the bubbling coffee, said quietly, "Yes, I've heard that version, but I don't believe it. Do you?"

Dolly was silent for a space, and then she muttered, "No." But she would say no more, and Jane, who was not inclined to press her, put the coffee onto a tray and carried it up to her room.

She settled herself comfortably and then took Allison's letters from her purse and read them carefully.

They were brief and said only what Allison had to say, without any sentimental padding. The first stated that Allison had heard that Dick had not taken the job, as he said he would. The second, dated only two days previously, announced her return to the town early the following morning and asked whether he was aware that he could never be entitled to Gloria's money.

CHAPTER 32

JANE STUDIED Allison's letters for some time, her forehead drawn into a perplexed little frown. In the second letter the word "never" was underlined. "You can never be entitled to Gloria's money!" Allison had known, then, that Jane was Gloria, and who but Dick could have told her? Yet in this letter she was telling Dick. It began to look as though someone else were in on the secret and had told Allison.

That "never" had a very final sound. Jane knew Allison well enough to realize that she was not referring to any moral issue. Such an angle would never have troubled Allison in the slightest, therefore she must have known of some legal obstacle.

Jane sighed on a long breath and was conscious that her head ached dully. She took two aspirins and stretched out on the bed, but it was some time before her exhaustion sent her into an uneasy doze.

Dolly woke her with a clattering dinner tray. "Gee, Missus," she said seriously, "you ought to see a doctor."

Jane piled pillows behind her and took the tray onto her lap. "Why?" she asked. "Is there an attractive one in town?"

"Nah," Dolly said. "Two old mossbacks and a young one with spectacles and a mouth full of teeth. But you been sick two nights now, and maybe you're comin' down with something."

"I am perfectly all right," Jane told her. "If someone had taken the trouble to wake me, I'd have come down to the dining room."

"Oh no, ma'am, you're sicker than you think," Dolly declared earnestly. "I heard Mister tell Chief Evinston he'd have to get the doctor's say-so before he could see you."

Jane began to laugh helplessly. Any number of people must have seen her in town this morning, and yet Evinston had to get permission from a doctor to ask her a few questions.

Dolly laughed, too, and presently took advantage of the bonhomous moment to ask whether it would be all right for her to go out after dinner to see a sick aunt.

Jane said, "Of course," and wondered why she bothered to ask, since the days of a maid being on twenty-four-hour duty were over.

"I just mentioned it," Dolly said cheerfully, "because Mrs. Mamie is fixing to clean out some closets tonight, and she told me I got to help her."

Jane smiled at Mamie's unbounded optimism, and Dolly laughed companiably. The laugh died away in mid-volume, however, when John appeared behind her and silently moved his head in unmistakable indication that Dolly was to get out. She got out, and Jane looked up at him with a glow of embarrassment burning in her face. It was really absurd, she thought helplessly, that she should be so constantly uneasy in his presence now.

His voice was clipped, and he was brief in what he had to say, and Jane wondered if she were mistaken in thinking that there was a faintly humorous expression in his eyes.

"Chief Evinston will be here shortly, and he's bringing Dr. Zentron. The doctor will give his considered opinion as to whether you are Gloria or not."

Jane nodded, shifted the tray on her lap, and could think of nothing to say.

"Naturally," John went on, "as soon as I agreed with the chief that you are not Gloria, he's all out to prove that you are. If the doctor decides that way, you might as well accept it, since you'll have to take your rightful place some time. As to the possible murder charge, I don't believe it will stick."

Jane shrugged and said almost indifferently, "I don't see how it can."

"Not as far as I can see now. Of course if there is something I don't know about, it may change the picture." He turned away and headed for the door. "I'll send Dolly up to let you know when they come."

After he had gone, Jane put the half-depleted tray away from her and wandered over to the window. The March landscape looked cold and bleak and added to her sense of absolute loneliness. If there were something that John did not know about? He must have meant that perhaps she had killed Allison, and, after all, he really didn't know. He'd known nothing about her when he married her. He seemed to have thrown her over completely, and she felt deserted by everyone. For a moment she felt that even her former life had been better than this, and then she gave her head an emphatic little shake. No, it had been no better. She was simply back where she had always been. She had to take care of herself with no help from anyone. It had been nice, though, to have John beside her and to know that he would always watch out for her. No use thinking about that now. It was over. She shed a few tears and then mopped at her eyes fiercely. Evinston and Dr. Zentron were coming, and she had to face them. She felt quite sure that the doctor would know her.

John did not send Dolly but brought the two men upstairs himself. The doctor looked at her steadily for a few moments, with the clear gray eyes that had always seemed to see through her as though she were made of glass. She gazed back in silence, and then the doctor turned abruptly and sent John and Evinston out of the room. He closed the door after them and then led Jane over to the window.

"Pull your hair away from your face."

Jane pulled it back, and he looked at her for a while and then said, "Now, let's see that mole."

She fumbled nervously at the neck of her dress and at last turned it down so that the mole was exposed. He bent to examine it.

"All right." He straightened up and pulled out his cigarette case. "Here, come and sit down."

He gave her a cigarette and sat close beside her on the edge of the bed, and when he spoke it was in a voice so low that only she could have heard it.

"I know Evinston has his big red ear flapping against the door. He's aching to make an arrest, even if it turns out to be wrong. He is not used to a murder like this, and his pride is smarting. It's the first time that he has not been able to arrest the guilty party within a few hours."

He paused to inhale deeply on his cigarette, and Jane wondered what he was leading up to.

"Now, it isn't going to be very pleasant for you if he decides to arrest you, so I suggest that I tell him I'm doing a few tests and will establish your identity, definitely, within a few days."

"You know who I am?"

He gave her one of those faint, superior, medical smiles, and said, "Of course, no question about it." He ran a professional finger over the bridge of her nose and murmured admiringly, "Made a good job of that. Who did it?"

Jane told him and added, "Most people seemed to be fooled about me, though."

"Most people observe nothing beyond the general effect. Now, about this amnesia business—"

She looked him straight in the eye and said nothing. She had a great deal of respect for his skill, and she doubted very much whether he could be misled on this issue, but, on the other hand, she was disinclined to admit anything until it was necessary.

He let it drop and went on to something else. "Of course Evinston is on a spot, anyway. If you are proved to be Gloria, it gives his cousin, who was the official in charge, a black eye for having closed the drowning case last summer, and he'll have to reopen it immediately and try to identify that other woman after all this time."

Jane took a long breath. "He'll still have to prove that I killed Allison too. He can't just say that I did it because he thinks so. And since I didn't do it, he'll have trouble proving it."

"Oh, as to that," the doctor said, "he figures on wringing a confession from you by his usual method—high pressure."

"I think I can resist that," Jane said firmly. "But I believe you ought to tell him who I am. He should find out the identity of that other poor girl. There may be relatives who are suffering because they don't know what has become of her."

Dr. Zentron shook his head. "Evinston's cousin is a shortsighted, stubborn mule. I told him repeatedly that that woman was not you, but he was determined to close the case. I felt impelled to make an investigation on my own, and it was comparatively easy, since the woman had made no effort to cover her tracks. As a matter of fact, I was about to take a trip to my shack in the mountains and make them open the case again. It must be done within a few days, in any event. She was just a derelict—a bar fly—although she had once been married to Dick Rouston."

CHAPTER 33

JANE WAS SILENT for a long moment, until her whirling thoughts settled a little.

"But that girl—" she stammered presently. "She didn't live around here anywhere. Dick divorced her some years ago, and I don't think he's even seen her since."

The doctor lifted his shoulders slightly and disposed of his cigarette. "He saw her when he identified her as you."

Jane frowned down at her hands, which were twisting nervously in her lap. "But I—I think you should tell Evinston. He ought to know. Dick's first wife drowned, and then someone pushed me over the bridge, and now Allison. He really should have that information."

"Evinston," said Dr. Zentron, "wouldn't know what to do with information if it were laid out before him, garnished with parsley and decorated with paper frills around its legs."

Jane was silent for a while, and then she said slowly, "Dick—surely he must have recognized that girl if she were his first wife."

"Not necessarily. He was a bit squeamish, and he hardly looked at her—left most of the identifying to the others. The officials were satisfied because they wanted to close the case and have done with it." Dr. Zentron got to his feet and smiled down at her. "Do you want me to hand in this information now, or wait until Evinston gets another suspect on his mind, so that he'll leave you alone?"

"Tell him now," Jane said decidedly. "It isn't fair to hold out on him."

"Ordinarily I'd agree with you, but in Evinston's case he's apt to get indigestion if you feed him too much information. It confuses him, and he can't think straight. If I keep you out of his grasp for a couple of days, he'll have to look around for someone else, and he might latch onto the right one."

"Do you know who the right one is?" Jane asked in a scared voice.

"No." He considered her for a moment and added, "Did you say that someone had pushed you over a bridge?"

Jane gave a nod that was accompanied by a little shudder. "Someone came up behind me. I never saw who it was, but I mean to find out."

"Well, that settles it," Dr. Zentron declared, and picked up his bag. "I'll tell the chief it will take a couple of days before I make up my mind as to your identity."

Jane shook her head. "I think it's wrong. He should have all the information we can give him. It's dangerous to cover things up."

Dr. Zentron chuckled and patted her on the head. "Sounds like Gloria all right—too honest. Absolute, forthright honesty can get you into trouble sometimes. Now I'm going to insist that you let things ride for a day or so. In the meantime, I'll do the investigating, and I have a lot more to go on than Evinston. I'm not going to have him arresting you simply because he can't think of anyone else."

Jane hung her head and said in a low voice, "How can you call me honest after what I have done?"

He laughed at her. "My dear child, you are quite typical. When the honest person decides to misbehave, he does it in a big way— does things the dishonest person wouldn't dare to do for fear he'd be found out." He patted her head again and left the room with a brisk step.

Jane got up from the bed and began to wander restlessly around the room. It seemed utterly fantastic. Dick's former wife drowned in that river in which she was supposed to have lost her own life, and at the same time.

Dick had never talked much about that first marriage. In fact, he'd been unusually reticent about it. She suddenly stopped and stared in front of her at nothing.

Allison's letter—the one in which she had said that Dick could never be entitled to the money—must have meant that Dick had not been properly divorced, and so he had never actually been married to Gloria and therefore had no claim to the money. Dick was a bigamist, like herself. Only, if they had never been married, then she wasn't a bigamist. She was John's wife. For a moment she felt a lifting of her spirits, but it died away again. John would want a divorce in any case.

She resumed her restless pacing and was conscious of a desire to go and tell John all about it, but she repressed it. He wasn't really interested. He was just trying to get out of the mess into which she had plunged him, without too much noise.

Her head was aching, and she stopped for a moment and pressed her palms against her forehead. She ought to go to Dick and ask him about that divorce. What must he have felt when he looked at the body and saw that it was his first wife? And then he calmly identified it as herself. But of course it had decomposed. Perhaps he hadn't recognized it after all. Dr. Zentron had identified it, though, and had found out all about her. How had he done it?

She undressed and went to bed, but she could not sleep. She began to think of the hot-air register and realized suddenly that the one in her room was in an entirely different position from the one downstairs in the drawing room. It had not struck her before, but obviously there could be no connection between the two. In that case, the music certainly had not come from the drawing room. It seemed likely that the pipe leading to her register came straight from the basement, and in all probability went on up to the third floor.

She got out of bed, thrust her feet into slippers, and pulled on a fleecy white robe which had been part of Jane's trousseau and could never have been selected by Gloria. She looked at the clock, saw that it was eleven-thirty, and sighed a little. It had been a long evening, and she had felt a desperate need to talk to someone.

She picked up her dinner tray and went out into the hall. She could see a light under John's closed door, but Mamie's room seemed to be in darkness. She went down to the kitchen, where she left the tray on a table, and then made her way to the drawing room. She satisfied herself that the register there had no connection with her room, and that therefore the music had come from somewhere else. She climbed the stairs again and after a few moments of nervous hesitation went on up to the third floor. She felt fairly certain that Dolly would not yet have returned from the tavern, since she rarely went to bed early, but she crept cautiously to the girl's room and tiptoed in without making a sound. There was enough light to show that the room was empty, but not enough for her to locate the hot-air register. She pressed the electric switch finally, although she knew that if Dolly were on her way home she'd be sure to see and identify the lighted window.

The room was untidy, with one bureau drawer and the door to the closet hanging open and Dolly's nightgown lying on the floor at the foot of the unmade bed. But Jane scarcely noticed these things, for she had found the hot-air register. It was directly over her own in the room below, and lying beside it she found her own portable phonograph with a small pile of records. They had been carelessly covered by an old automobile rug.

CHAPTER 34

SO DOLLY HAD a hand in this grim business, Jane thought. But how? And why? She had always known that Dolly was not to be trusted. There was something sly about her. She rubbed a clenched fist across her forehead and felt that it was all getting to be too much for her. She was tired and confused, and there seemed to be no one to help her.

She looked through the records and found that they were mostly the recordings of her own playing, which were not good enough to interest anyone but herself. There were a few others, some classical pieces that she had liked and had played in the privacy of her own room. She remembered that they had all been together in a case, and apparently Dolly had simply picked up the case and brought it here.

She put one of her own recordings onto the little phonograph and then ran downstairs to her room. The sound was exactly as she had heard it before—a ghostly, faraway melody. She went upstairs again, removed the record and replaced it, and draped the rug over the whole thing just as she had found it. She switched off the light and went slowly downstairs, feeling tired and dispirited. She was tired of the whole thing, she thought wearily—Pete Hoge stealing Rose's ring and having it reset, Allison writing that Dick had no claim on her money, Dolly trying to scare her out of her home with ghostly music.

Her home. If only it *were* her home and all these other people and her former life could be blotted out.

She slipped back into her own room and immediately went rigid with shock. John was there, standing by the window, neatly wrapped up in the robe he had bought for his wedding and had never worn because it was too warm. His eyebrows were drawn together in an angry frown, and he looked at her as though she were an employee who was about to be fired.

Jane sighed and was conscious of the old feeling of being an outcast, but she'd known it for so long that she was used to it. She looked at him in silence and waited for him to speak.

"Why are you running all over the house at this time of night?" he asked furiously.

"Why, I—" She started to tell him all about it, but he interrupted her.

"You're up to something, and I intend to know what it is. I won't have you creeping around on your own secret affairs in this house. If you find out anything new in this miserable business, you're to tell me at once and keep out of it yourself. The sooner it's cleared up, the better it will be all around, but you'd better get it out of your head that you can do it single-handed. The fact that you've been sneaking around means that you're on the track of something, or you think you are, and I want an immediate explanation."

Jane, who had been so subdued for so long, suddenly lost her temper. It was a surprise, even to herself, and although she tried to keep her voice calm, it came out high and shrill. "And suppose I don't choose to explain?"

"Then you can pack up and get out," he said curtly.

Her first impulse was to do just that—to pack up and get out, and never see or speak to John again. But she remembered the fruitless excursion with Gus, and instead she said hotly, "Oh no, I shall stay here. If anyone goes, it will be you."

He was considerably taken aback and showed it. She had been so reasonable before this, penitent and quiet, doing what she was told without question. He wondered if she were beginning to show her true colors, and his voice was ominous as he asked quietly, "What makes you think you can stay here if I decide to put you out?"

"I *am* your wife. It has developed that I never was married to Dick, and so my marriage with you is legal. Unless, of course, you have an excess wife hanging around somewhere."

She began to be a little afraid of her own boldness. She was not at all sure of her facts. This was merely something that she had settled in her own mind, and she was very far from being able to prove it.

John was obviously startled. He was silent for some time, his eyes on her white, exhausted face, and then he picked up a cigarette and sat down in the only chair that the room held.

"Get into bed," he said briefly, "and tell me what you mean."

Jane exchanged the fleecy white robe for the tailored bed jacket and slipped in between the sheets. She started a cigarette of her own, and resting her head against the pillows, was uneasily silent. She did not want to explain anything further. She had said too much as it was.

"Come on," John urged impatiently. "Surely I deserve an explanation of a statement like that."

"Well—" Jane drew a long, unsteady breath. "Of course this is mostly inference on my part, but I'm quite sure that I'm right."

He listened intently while she told him what Dr. Zentron had said and about Allison's letters, and when she had finished he said rather dryly, "You think that proves that Dick was never divorced from the woman? I don't think he's that much of a fool."

"He isn't—I know that—but I believe the divorce was a false one. Dr. Zentron was able to unearth some facts, and Allison picked up some information somewhere. She told her aunt she was coming up here to force me to give up my husband."

John raised his eyebrows, "She meant me, then."

"You?" Jane looked puzzled for a moment, and then her face cleared. If Allison knew that Dick was not her husband, and that, therefore, John was, she must have been referring to John. "When did you see Allison?" she asked quickly.

"Only once—just a glimpse of her. Rose told me who it was."

"Then she saw you, and she approved of you, but she wasn't really after you. You see, I know how her mind worked. She was after the money, and she came here to make a deal with me. I was to give up the money and she would leave you alone. It would not have occurred to her that she couldn't get you if she wanted you, and she had good reason to think so, too. She'd always been able to pick up any man she wanted. She had such confidence in herself."

Jane seemed to be talking as much to herself now as to him, and John said nothing when she paused with a faraway look in her eyes. Certainly she knew all these people, and perhaps she was on the right track. Perhaps the wretched pall of misery that had hung over this house was going to be lifted at last.

"Allison had found out that Dick was not divorced," Jane went on, "so that he was not entitled to my money."

"If you had made a will—"

Jane looked up at him. "Oh yes, but she knew that I was Gloria too, and she certainly knew that I wouldn't marry Dick again."

"How did she know that you were Gloria?"

"I think Dick knew me almost from the first," Jane said slowly, "and he told Allison. She never was one to sit down and wonder what to do next, so she came home and made up her mind to blackmail me."

"You think that was her reason for coming to this house?" John asked. "How did she get in?"

"Through that broken window. I think she was familiar with it, because she had been meeting Dick here secretly; and I believe the note that Evinston found was an old one. Perhaps she dropped it when she came in some time, and it lodged in the shutter, or something of that sort. But this last time she intended to find me, and threaten—"

"Now wait a minute," John interrupted impatiently. "You think the girl came through that window and intended to walk upstairs, knock on a door, hoping it was yours, and ask if she could speak to you for a minute, and all this after midnight?"

Jane thought it over for a while, and then opened her eyes very wide.

"Oh no. I see now. This time she came to see Dolly."

CHAPTER 35

JOHN STOOD UP abruptly and walked over to the window, where he looked blankly out into the darkness. There was a long silence, and then he swung around again and went to stand at the foot of Jane's bed.

"This is fantastic," he said quietly. "I think you've allowed your imagination to run away with you."

"It's fantastic that Allison was killed in this house, and I've no doubt it has a fantastic explanation."

He jammed his hands into the pockets of his robe and asked almost belligerently, "Can you think up any shred of a reason why Allison would come here for a secret conference with Dolly?"

"No, I can't." Jane looked at him squarely, with her chin raised a little. "But that doesn't prove that there isn't one. Anyway, it looks as though Allison had been killed before she ever got to Dolly."

"I'll have Dolly up on the mat," John decided suddenly, "and find out whether she had any business with Allison."

"Oh no, you, can't do it that way. She wouldn't tell you anything. She'd only close up tight. I know Dolly, and I know that she doesn't tell things directly. She drops little hints while she's talking about other things. If you leave her alone she'll eventually let it out by herself."

John set his jaw, and said, "No. She'll answer me, and she'll answer me now."

Jane sighed. "She won't answer you now, because she isn't home yet."

But in the brief silence that followed they both heard the distant slam of the back door, and presently Dolly's footsteps could be heard quietly mounting the stairs. John turned without a word and left the room, and Jane could hear his voice in the hall, clipped and sharp. He returned almost immediately with Dolly sidling along behind him, her eyes wary and a little frightened.

"I'm sorry about gettin' home so late," she offered breathlessly, "but my aunt was awful sick, and when she's like that, she don't want no one but me with her, so I had to sit there—"

"Don't bother, Dolly," Jane said quietly, "we really don't care how late you come in."

John made an impatient movement with his arm. "I merely want to know what business Miss Allison Ketria had with you on the night she was killed in this house."

Dolly denied it to high heaven volubly, with her eyes rolling, and Jane knew that that angle was hopeless, at least for the present. She interrupted the loud protestations by saying in a clear, firm voice, "Dolly, how did you find out that those records of my piano playing could be heard in this room when they were played in yours?"

"I had one playin' up there," Dolly said vaguely, "and then I had to run down to the front door. I forgot I left it on and went into your room to do my cleanin'. Before you come, that was, and I could hear the pianner playin'—sort of faint and ghostly. I was so scared I nearly swallowed my gum, until I remembered I'd left the phonograph goin' up in my room!"

She seemed unconscious of having given herself away, and Jane could not resist a quick glance of triumph at John. She kept her voice low and impersonal and asked Dolly almost carelessly, "When did you first realize that I was Gloria?"

"I never thought of such a thing at first," Dolly said abstractedly, as though she were speaking as much to herself as to Jane. "It was when you started playin' that pianner they sent over. I couldn't miss your playin'. I like the pianner, and I play myself. I came to the door and looked at you, and I couldn't make head or tail to it—seemed as though it must be a ghost. I was all upset and scared, and I ruined the dinner. I kept lookin' at you all the time after that, and pretty soon I began to see it really was you."

Jane gave an easy little laugh. "It was quite a joke, wasn't it? Who did you tell first, about my being Gloria, I mean?"

But it had started to dawn on Dolly that she'd been doing a lot of talking, and she merely eyed Jane rather wildly in silence.

"Did you tell it around at the tavern?"

Dolly was shocked into speech. "No, ma'am, I wouldn't of told it to that bunch of— Oh no, I went over and told Miss Sally, she being your only blood kin, see."

Jane nodded. "Of course, that was the right thing to do. What did Sally say?"

"She wouldn't believe me. Told me I was always gettin' what she called wild ideas and said for me not to be a fool."

"She must have felt pretty silly," Jane said casually, "when she found out that she was wrong and you were right'"

"Yeah," said Dolly, "only she ain't found it out yet. Leastways, she ain't sayin' so, even now, when practically everyone knows it."

John stirred and asked, "Do you mean the whole town knows it with the exception of the Roustons?"

Dolly's voice reflected her fear of John, but she answered readily enough, "Oh, sure, they're all talkin' about it, and sayin' the Roustons are sitting tight so they can hang onto the money."

"And," Jane supplied, "that I killed Allison in a fit of jealousy."

"Yeah," Dolly agreed, without embarrassment, "that's what they all think."

'But you know better, don't you?" Jane asked.

Dolly gave her, an amiable smile. "Oh, sure. Them punks don't know you like I do. The way I figure it, someone else musta done it."

"Then why," asked Jane quickly, "were you trying to frighten me by playing those records?"

Dolly removed the smile and dropped her eyes to a point somewhere below Jane's chin. She said uneasily, "That that was just a joke, see."

"Oh no it wasn't." The casual ease was gone from Jane's voice, and she added sharply, "You told someone about the ghostly sound of the music in this room, and you were instructed to play those records at night, perhaps in an effort to frighten me into insanity."

Dolly backed away a step and sent a scared glance between the two of them. "I—no—I don't remember—"

John snapped, "You'll tell us at once, or I'll take you down to Evinston's office and let him drag it out of you."

"I don't know anything about it, any of this," Dolly protested in a terrified whimper. "I tell you, I don't know no more than you do about it."

"But you know who told you to play those records," John said angrily.

Dolly began to deny everything in a whining jumble of words, and Jane half closed her eyes and tried to think it out. Dolly certainly would not be making any social calls over at the other house, and so one of them must have come here. Dick, of course. He had come over frequently to inspect the furnace, and Dolly would never tell on Dick. The chances were that he had turned a languid but admiring eye on her from time to time.

"Dolly," she said suddenly, "I appreciate your sense of loyalty, but it's all right to tell me, because, you see, I know anyway. It was Mr. Rouston, wasn't it? It was he you let in the front door when you left the phonograph playing, and when you discovered that it could be heard in this bedroom, you told him right away. Isn't that so?"

Dolly's mouth had dropped open, and there was a look of awe on her face. She nodded mutely.

"And then, after I had arrived and Mr. Rouston had sent over my old piano, you told him that I was Gloria, and he asked you to play the records in the middle of the night, just for a joke."

"Yeah," Dolly said, with a sort of feverish relief. "Yeah, that was it—just a joke." She gave John's set face a terrified glance and then fell to studying blindly the catch on her battered purse.

Jane wished that he would relax a bit or, better still, go away and leave them alone. She knew how to manage Dolly, but the woman's fear of John made everything a great deal more difficult.

She looked at Dolly and said mildly, "Why did you always close the drawing-room doors when you played that joke on me?"

"Why, I didn't," Dolly said in some surprise, and speaking more naturally. "Maybe they was shut sometimes. I been trying to get them to work smooth, and I hadda open and close them some. I got some stuff for doors like that, kinda oily, but I loaned it to Mr. Dick, and he never give it back. I went over to look for it, but—" Her voice trailed away, and she dropped her eyes in some confusion.

If the "kinda oily" stuff was what she had been after in Dick's room, Jane reflected, it was innocent enough.

John made an impatient movement, and Jane said quickly, "I do wish I knew why Allison came to see you that night. Haven't you any idea about it?"

But Dolly, still agitatedly working, on the clasp of her purse, would not be drawn any further. She knew little or nothing about Allison Ketria, could conceive of nothing that the girl might have had to say to her, and, in fact, did not believe that there had been anything.

Jane, watching the restless hands as they clasped and unclasped the worn purse, suddenly drew her breath sharply.

Dolly wore a large diamond on her engagement finger, and Jane immediately connected it with the one Pete Hoge had taken to the jeweler that morning.

CHAPTER 36

JOHN STARTED TO SAY something, but Jane broke in on him and asked quickly, "Dolly, why did Mr. Hoge give you that ring?"

Dolly's busy hands became still, and with a hasty movement of her left thumb she slid the diamond around to her palm.

"Come on," Jane said impatiently, when she remained silent. "You'd better tell, or you'll get into trouble. If you don't explain to us, Evinston will certainly wring it out of you, so you might as well break down now and avoid all that fuss."

Dolly swallowed convulsively and seemed unable to speak, and John looked from one to the other of them, half puzzled and half angry. He knew nothing about the ring and had no idea of what Jane was getting at.

But Jane's entire attention was fixed on Dolly. She asked softly, "Are you engaged to Pete Hoge?"

Dolly found her voice and used it in shrill denial. "No—oh no—of course not."

"Then why are you wearing his ring on the third finger of your left hand?"

Dolly looked helplessly down at her finger, where only the gold band of the ring now showed. "I—I just wore it on that finger—just tonight—it was to fool someone."

Jane released a long breath and dropped her head against the pillow. At least she had established that the ring had come from Pete.

"You'd better tell me why he gave it to you," she said after a moment and tried to keep her face properly grave as she added the punch line, "or, you'll have to tell Evinston."

"Well—but it ain't anything—it don't mean nothing," Dolly muttered.

"You can let us judge as to what it means," John said curtly.

Dolly gave him a sidelong look that was full of fear and then glanced over her shoulder at the door behind her. John followed the glance and took a step toward her, and she cried out, "It wasn't nothing—just something he didn't want me to tell."

"What?"

Dolly closed her eyes and said in a voice of despair, "He'll take the ring back if I tell."

John laid a hand on her arm. "I'm tired of trying to drag things out of you. You'll go with me to Chief Evinston now, if we have to get him out of bed."

"No, wait a minute," Dolly cried hysterically, "I'll tell, but you got to promise you won't tell it was me."

"I'll make no promises of any sort," John retorted. "You can tell us or not as you like, but make up your mind quickly because I don't intend to stand around here all night."

"It was that woman," Dolly said desperately. "Came to the front door and said she was Mr. Rouston's wife, and she wanted to see him."

"When was this?" John asked sharply.

Dolly had to clear her throat twice before she replied faintly, "Summer—last summer when we was all up in the country there. She come early in the morning, and I opened the door, but Mr. Hoge was up, and he heard us, and he come flying to the door and pushed me away—said he'll take care of it. I wouldn't of paid any attention if he hadn't of been in such a stew, but I went into the dining room and listened. Anyways, Mr. Hoge, he told her she wasn't married to Mr. Rouston, and she claimed she was—said she found out the mail-order divorce wasn't no good, and Mr. Hoge said certainly it was good, and she didn't have a leg to stand on. She up and told him the divorce was as phony as his two front teeth—Mr. Pete lost them teeth in an accident and had to have store ones put in—and if she didn't get to see Mr. Dick, she'd make a lot of trouble. So Mr. Pete sort of backed down and said Mr. Dick wasn't at home, but he'd fix a meeting between them, and she finally went away. So then Mr. Pete came out and found me, and says I wasn't to mention it to no one. Said he'd wait a while, and if it didn't leak out, and nobody heard of it, I'd get a swell present."

"So you got the ring," Jane said, "even though you told Allison Ketria."

Dolly denied it vociferously. "I never told no one, not one soul." But the color had drained out of her face.

"Then how did she find out?" John asked.

"I don't know, sir," Dolly said. "I don't know nothing about it. Anyways, how do you know she knew?"

"Don't you think," Jane suggested, "that you should clear yourself by telling us why she came to see you that night?"

But Dolly began to stammer and deny again, and took two more backward steps toward the safety of the door.

"You know perfectly well why she came to see you," John said sternly. "Now stop wasting time and tell us."

Dolly broke into tears. "I'm tired," she sobbed. "It's late and I need my sleep. I work hard all day, and I got to get my sleep at night. And anyways, I don't know anything more to tell you."

John looked her over in silence and then said abruptly, "Go to bed. But I'm warning you that you'll either give that information to me in the morning or you'll give it to Evinston."

Dolly was gone almost before he had stopped speaking, and when the door had closed behind her, he lit a cigarette and was silent for a while, his head bent a little, and the smoke drifting up. Presently he looked up at Jane and said rather abruptly that he'd see her in the morning.

She was surprised to hear her own voice asking, "What shall we do if we find that we really are married, after all?"

"Get a divorce," he said curtly, and made for the door. He opened it and then paused long enough to tell her to stay where she was and not to start running around the house again.

After he had gone, Jane lay and gloomed up at the ceiling. She wondered what had possessed her to ask the question and realized that she had been hoping for another answer. She brushed aside the thought that Dick's divorce might have been in order. She didn't want it that way. She wanted to be married to John.

He was set against her now, though. It was obvious that he wanted nothing more to do with her, but she could not quite give up a faint little hope that he would come back to her in spite of everything.

Suddenly into the silence of the room there came the faint sound of a piano playing. Jane sat straight up in bed. What did Dolly think she was doing, anyway, playing that phonograph when it no longer meant anything? She had said she was dead tired and needed sleep.

Jane got out of bed in a fit of impatience. She was tired beyond telling of the sound of those piano pieces, and she'd put a stop to it at once.

She put on the white robe, went quietly into the hall, and up the attic stairs. She found her way to Dolly's room without bumping into anything and discovered that the door was ajar and the room in darkness. There was a brilliant moon outside, and it gave enough light to show her that Dolly was not there. As she hesitated, the record came to an end, and the mechanism turned off of itself.

On a sudden impulse Jane went to the window and looked out over the moonlit fields below.

She could see a flying figure, which she identified as Dolly, hurrying frantically in the direction of the Rouston house.

CHAPTER 37

JANE LEFT Dolly's room and went downstairs and straight to John's door, where she knocked sharply. She heard him stir and then get out of bed and cross the floor. He opened the door and looked out at her, and she wondered for a moment whether he would ever again look at her with anything but cold dislike.

She said quietly, "Dolly is rushing over to the Rouston house. I saw her, and I want to find out who she is contacting. I'm going to follow her, but I thought I'd better let you know. I—" Her voice trailed away, and she began to regret having spoken to him at all. There was no reason for it, really. She should just have gone by herself and said nothing to anyone.

But John had already turned back into the room and was throwing on some clothes. "I'll go," he said shortly. "You stay here."

"She was playing one of those records again," Jane explained, "probably so that I would think she was in her room."

He made no reply, and she thought of the keys to the Rouston house which she had in her purse. She went and got them and handed them to him with a brief explanation as he was starting down the stairs. He nodded and dropped them into his pocket, and after he had gone she went to one of the back windows and watched him as he cut across the fields. Dolly was no longer in sight, and she thought uneasily that she should have gone herself, since she knew the house better. But once she had aroused him, it would have been futile to insist. John was determined, and he had a strong sense of duty. It had been different with Dick. She'd had to do everything herself, except open doors or light her cigarettes. In fact, with Dick everything had to be done by someone else while he distributed thanks charmingly and reclined on the end of his spine. She could not imagine him, either, being cold and distant for days on end because he had found out that she had married him bigamously. He'd have laughed in genuine amusement, even at first, when he was still pretending to be in love with her, and would have made some humorous comment about keeping it quiet because it wouldn't look right to the neighbors. But it looked now as though it might be the other way around. If Dick's divorce had not been legal, then he'd married her bigamously.

She found that she was shivering, and she went back to bed and pulled the blankets up around her shoulders. She lit a cigarette, and lay smoking and looking absently up at the ceiling.

That divorce of Dick's—there was something—they had never discussed it much, because she'd disliked his having been a divorcé, but he had told her about it, and there was something else— Oh yes, Pete Hoge. Pete had been detailed to look into the divorce and see that it was all in order. He'd been hanging around Rose even then. It was before her husband had been killed, but he had already gone off to the war. And now Pete was hanging around Betsy, and had given that ring to Dolly.

Jane had a moment of utter confusion, which she put aside firmly. After all, she knew these people, and she should be able to figure it out.

The ring had been given to Dolly in the form of hush money, and it had been lying in Rose's bureau drawer among a collection of rubbish. Rose had always been extremely careful with her good jewelry, and so there was only one answer to that. The stone was not a diamond but something far less valuable, and Pete Hoge knew it but Dolly did not.

What was Pete up to, anyway? Intrigue was not down his alley at all. He was just a hanger-on to people who were smarter than himself. And how could he possibly have raised enough courage and independence to pay court to Betsy with Rose looking on? He couldn't, so it followed that either Rose had cast him off and he was getting even with her, or he was carrying out her private instructions. Not the former, though, because Rose was ambitious for Betsy, and she would have put a stop to it at once. So he was doing what Rose had told him to do. But what was her reason? And why did Betsy respond to a man so much older than herself? Well, that was understandable, perhaps. These young girls liked to have an older beau. But Betsy had been very fond of a young boy in the local high school, the grocer's son, and Rose had thought she was seeing too much of him. What was his name? Bill—that was it. Rose had been quite disturbed about it, and it was one of the reasons she'd wanted Betsy sent to a private school. She'd said more than once that she wanted the friendship broken up. Of course that was the explanation. It was as simple as that. Rose had sent Pete to cut Bill out with Betsy, one job that he was thoroughly capable of doing well. Bill was easily disposed of, and then all Pete had to do was to keep Betsy interested until Rose was ready to pack her off to school.

Jane crushed out her cigarette and slid deeper into the warmth of the blankets. Well, that was that, but it cast no light on the murder of Allison Ketria. Dolly, she thought, must have gone flying over to the Roustons' to tell Pete that things were getting a bit hot. It would almost have to be Pete she'd gone to see—Pete, who'd paid her bounty in the form of an imitation diamond. He must be the outer fence for someone else, for Rose, probably. He'd belonged to Rose for so long. It was odd that she'd never married him. No, it wasn't. Actually, it was very simple. Money. Pete had none, and Rose really had to have money. She'd been without it for so long. It seemed clear enough when you looked back on it. If only Gloria were out of the way, Dick would see to it that Rose had enough money to marry Pete. She had wanted Pete, too. No doubt about that.

Jane moved her head restlessly on the pillow. She herself had never had the craving for money that seemed to torment the rest of them. And Rose had been more tormented even than the others.

It would have been so easy for Rose to push Gloria over the bridge and solve the problem. But she must have pushed that other poor creature over first—Dick's former wife. Well, probably she had, and perhaps Dolly had seen her do it, or she might have seen her when she pushed Gloria over. No, that didn't sound right. If Dolly had seen anything, the chances were that Dolly would have gone over the bridge too. Nor could Pete have known anything about it, or he'd have been so terrified that he'd have run away long before this.

So it was Rose's secret, and it must have been a grim burden, especially when only one body was recovered instead of two. And then one day Dolly came panting to the house with the news that young Mrs. Cowrer was really Gloria. Rose would have instantly labeled it rubbish and nonsense, but Dolly was very sure, and Rose began to give her presents and a little money to hold her tongue. She still refused to believe the tale, insisting that it was impossible to identify a person by the way she played the piano, but Dolly agreed to say nothing as soon as the first present and a little money were in her hands along with a vague promise of more to come.

Then Rose, in some fashion, came upon Allison's letter to Dick and realized that Allison intended to air the whole matter thoroughly before she married him. It wouldn't stand airing, and Rose knew it.

The first wife must have been threatening to make trouble in the hope of picking up some money. Rose knew the divorce was not legal, but she had instructed Pete to declare that it was quite valid, and he had done as he was told. It must have been a bad moment for Rose when the woman turned up while they were staying up in the mountains. Probably she had arranged a meeting on the bridge. The woman had been troublesome and nasty, and Rose had given her the fatal push on angry impulse. It had been so easy and uncomplicated that later she had not been able to resist sending Gloria over too. There would be no real freedom for her until the money belonged to Dick.

Rose could not have known about Dr. Zentron's investigation. All she knew was that Allison was on her way to confer with Dolly, and Dolly knew too much.

The troublesome fog had cleared away now, and Jane understood it all.

Dolly had not been able to resist letting Allison know that Dick had never been married to Gloria, by her usual method of dropping hints, and Allison had demanded an interview to get the whole story. Dolly agreed but insisted that it be late at night, with Allison coming through the broken window and going all the way up to Dolly's room, so that no one could know there had been a meeting between them. But Allison must have talked somewhere, at some time, because Rose was there before her.

No doubt Rose had tried to convince the girl that everything was all right, and a discussion with Dolly unnecessary—and failed utterly. The murder followed, more violent, this time, and less cautious.

Jane wondered a little why she had not gone up and murdered Dolly too, then shuddered at the thought. That would be too much, even for Rose. Besides, she had probably figured that Dolly would come in handy as a suspect. She wouldn't be capable of putting up much of a defense.

It was clear now, too, why Dick had told Dolly to play the records. Dolly had gone flying over to them with the news that Mrs. Cowrer played the piano so like Gloria that she must be Gloria, and Dick, acting independently, had told her to produce the ghostly music in the hope that it might frighten Gloria away. The records, of course, explained why the black piano played of itself while it was still at the big house. It was up in the attic, and so were Dolly and the phonograph.

Jane suddenly felt her body go rigid with a new fear. Rose would have to kill her next. It was the only way. Why, she must have started—must be coming now—to make a second murderous attempt to get Gloria out of the way forever.

CHAPTER 38

JANE, SHIVERING under her blankets, tried to tell herself that her imagination was getting out of control, but there was a deadly feeling of certainty within her. Would Pete be at the Rouston house now? Probably he was. He often stayed there. Dolly would rouse him and breathlessly repeat what had just passed between herself and the Cowrers, and Pete would tell her to go back home and keep her mouth shut. Then Pete would go quietly and report to Rose and would be told, in his turn, to go back to bed and keep his mouth shut. When he was safely out of the way, Rose would dress quickly and sneak out, just missing John.

Jane turned restlessly in the bed and wished that she could stop shivering. The house was so utterly still, and she could not reason away the terror that had her heart pounding against her ribs.

Suddenly she was quite still, her head raised a little from the pillow and her ears straining. There was someone walking quietly up the stairs. The stealthy footsteps reached the top, approached her door, and hesitated. Jane stopped breathing altogether, and then the footsteps went on, and she heard them going up to the attic.

In a panting flood of relief Jane realized that it was Dolly, and that was how she had figured it out too. Pete had sent her back home and told her to go to bed. Rose would be due in another ten or fifteen minutes.

Jane stretched a shaking hand to the cigarette box on the bedside table and broke two matches in her fumbling fingers before she was able to get a light.

Perhaps John would get back first, she thought, and knew with despairing certainty that he would not. He would arouse the entire house and insist on getting to the bottom of everything, because that was John's way. And he would not find Rose missing because Dick would cover up for her. Only Rose wouldn't come, if she knew that John was there. She'd have to wait, but if she missed John and did not know that he was there, then certainly she would come. She must know by now that the Cowrers were sleeping in separate rooms.

Dolly, the town crier, must have spread it far and wide by this time.

Did Rose believe the amnesia story? Whether she did or not, she'd have let things slide if they were going all right, but they were not going right now and she'd have to act.

She must be close—downstairs at the door—no, not the door—at the long window that would not lock.

Jane, got out of bed and pulled on the white robe with clammy, shaking hands. She'd go out and listen for her, and face her. It would be no use phoning Chief Evinston. He'd only tell her she'd been having nightmares.

She looked vaguely around for something with which she could protect herself, but there did not seem to be anything. In the end she picked up a hairbrush and went out into the hall feeling both terrified and silly.

There was no sound to break the awful silence. Everything seemed to be waiting. She looked down the stairwell into blackness and began to descend slowly, one step at a time. By the time she got to the bottom she was shivering, and she could feel a cold draft of air on her face. She knew at once that it came from the long window, standing open now while Rose crept around, or waited, somewhere in the blackness of that lower floor.

Jane pulled the fleecy material of her robe closer around her neck and advanced a few cautious, shaking steps. She must be careful. It was too dark to see anything, and Rose was here somewhere.

The silence was broken by a faint whispering of silk somewhere off to her right, and she backed up, feeling for the wall behind her and trying to fight the panic that was seeping into her control. She wanted to get back to the stairs but, as she started to turn, something crashed down on her head and she knew it was too late.

The darkness burst into a galaxy of brilliant rockets, and she was conscious, as she fell, of a rather mournful feeling of regret. She should have been more careful, only she hadn't quite believed her own deductions. Her head would be battered to a pulp. The whole thing was infinitely sad but oddly peaceful. She tried to bring her arm around to protect her head, but she seemed to be lying on it, and then the rockets went out, and she slid into darkness.

It seemed to be much later that she heard Mamie's excited voice and became conscious of an irritated wish that people would leave her head alone. Someone was holding her hand in a warm, strong grip, and water was running somewhere. The water was shut off abruptly, and then she heard John's voice.

"Mamie, for God's sake be quiet."

Jane opened her eyes. There was that lamp on the bedside table that she liked so, only it didn't give very much light. She could see Mamie at the foot of the bed, but where was John? She glanced down at her hand, still held so firmly in that warm grip, and saw that it was John holding it. She raised her eyes, realized that he was sitting by her bed, and was at once wrapped in a peaceful content.

John removed his hand when he saw that her eyes were open and looked a bit self-conscious. Her head was aching, but she felt a giggle pushing up into her throat, and she said, quite clearly, "I saw you."

John looked at her for a moment and then said in a worried voice, "Mamie! You'd better get the doctor back. She's delirious."

"She's nothing of the sort," Mamie said comfortably. "You heard what the doctor said. It's only a slight concussion at the worst. But the poor child has had a nasty shock, and I'll bet she has a headache fit to knock her hat off. What she wants is a little sympathy."

Jane, with all the inhibitions temporarily knocked out of her, grinned up at him. John pushed his chair back about a foot, and Mamie laughed derisively.

"Give him time," she said cheerfully to Jane. "He always was a slowpoke and a stuffed shirt, but you can depend on him to the last ditch. Well, I'll have to get on with the job of clearing up the mess the doctor left. I never knew one yet who didn't spew things all over the room for someone else to pick up. They're so used to the nurses waiting on them, I guess."

"Was Dr. Zentron here?" Jane asked wonderingly.

"Certainly was." Mamie chuckled. "Also that hole in the doughnut, Chief Evinston. He wanted to know what kind off an illness it was kept you from seeing him and still allowed you to run all over town yesterday." She paused for a moment and her face sobered. "I suppose you know who hit you?"

John said sharply, "Mamie! Please!"

Jane closed her aching eyes. "It's all right. I know. She had to do it."

"Why?" John asked quickly. "No one else seems to know."

"Didn't she tell?"

"She can't," John said quietly. "She's dead."

CHAPTER 39

THEY WERE IN the drawing room, Jane sitting in an armchair and John at the window, while Mamie flitted about chatting brightly of nothing. All the books were still piled up on the floor, waiting for the shelves that John had been going to build for them. Perhaps he never would build them now, Jane thought.

They were to have a conference with Dick, and Jane heartily wished that it were over. She thought of Rose with a shudder and wondered whether she'd ever be able to get the thing entirely out of her mind. How awful it must be to want money with such a morbid craving as Rose had had. She hadn't really been a killer to start with. She hadn't killed that woman, Dick's first wife, in cold blood. They knew now, because she had told Dick all about it after Jane and John had appeared in town and Dolly had come over with the news that Jane was Gloria. The woman had been attempting blackmail, and Rose had intercepted a note that she had sent to Dick, so that Rose had met her on the rustic bridge. The woman had become abusive and had eventually attacked Rose, and during the ensuing struggle she had gone over the railing accidentally, simply disappearing into the water. Rose could not help realizing what a simple solution it was. A few days later she had come upon Gloria leaning on the railing of the bridge. The temptation to solve all their problems in such an easy fashion had been too much. But Rose had not told Dick about that, nor about the more violent murder of Allison, and his accusation of Jane was honest enough. Rose had talked to him after that, and had, in her own words, tried to put sense into his head. It was probable that he had begun to suspect her at about that time, although he said nothing.

Rose had taken her own gun to the rendezvous with Allison, a large, old-fashioned thing that had belonged to her father, but even in her anger she feared that a shot could be traced back to her, and so she had used it as a bludgeoning weapon.

She knew all the time that Gloria, even in her role as Jane, was a constant menace and would have to be dealt with eventually. John could only surmise things, but Gloria knew—knew that she had been pushed over the bridge. So Rose had made a last desperate effort and it had failed. John had seen her leave the Rouston house while he was trying to get in and had followed her. He had not been in time to stop the first blow, but he had intercepted the killing blows that were to have followed. Rose had wrenched herself away from him and had gone as far as the veranda, where she turned the gun upon herself on impulse. They always did things on impulse. If she had stopped to think at all, she might have tried insanity as a defense, or something of the sort.

"Here he comes," John said.

Jane looked up. "Who?"

John merely looked at her, and she colored and said hastily, "Oh yes, Dick. I was thinking of something else."

"It might do you a lot of good," John observed mildly, "to stop thinking altogether for a while."

Mamie had gone to the door and proceeded to usher Dick into the drawing room. She tried to slide quietly into a chair, but John, after nodding briefly to Dick, gave her a meaningful look and gestured toward the door.

"I won't say a word," Mamie said pleadingly. "You won't even notice me."

John merely said, "I'm sorry," and after a brief silence Mamie got up and flounced out. John closed the sliding doors firmly behind her.

Dick looked awful, Jane thought. His eyes were sunken in his head, and his face had a tight, drawn appearance. He sat facing her, and John took a chair beside him so that they were both looking at her. Jane looked at her feet and wished that she were anywhere else.

"Well," John said, after an uncomfortable silence. .

"There's nothing to say," Dick muttered. "Except that I have packed and am ready to go. I'm here to find out what is to become of Sally."

"I shall make her an allowance," Jane said quickly.

Dick nodded. "Is she to live with you?"

"No!" Jane spoke sharply, and then dropped her eyes to her twisting hands and added more gently, "I'll make the allowance sufficient for her to live separately."

Dick's haggard face brightened a little, and he stood up. "I'll tell her. I know she wants to leave as soon as possible, and Betsy can stay with her until I make other arrangements."

Jane dropped her head against the back of her chair and closed her eyes as John ushered Dick out with cold formality.

So she was still supporting them. Only she didn't really mind now. She would not have to live with them. Sally would undoubtedly share her home with Dick as well as Betsy, but that was up to Sally.

She heard John come back into the room and close the sliding doors after him with a firm click. He walked over to her chair, and she opened her eyes and looked up at him.

"They're moving within the hour," he told her. "You could move over there this afternoon, if you wanted to."

She nodded and asked quietly, "When do you want to start the divorce?"

He put his hands into his pockets, regarded his shoes for a moment, and then said slowly, "I've been thinking about that. For business reasons I'd prefer not to have it now."

"In that case," Jane replied carefully, "I'd better not move into the big house just now, because then everybody would know that we were separated."

He glanced up at her. "It would be nice of you, if you would stay for a while."

Jane smiled at him. "I'll be glad to stay and help you out," she said, and realized with sudden amusement that at the moment they were leading figures in the biggest scandal the town had ever known.

John leaned down, pulled her to her feet, and put his arm around her.

"Dolly and Mamie," he said in an undertone, "are directly outside the door, ready and waiting to spread the news around town, so I'd better kiss you."

THE END

About The Rue Morgue Press

The Rue Morgue vintage mystery line is designed to bring back into print those books that were favorites of readers between the turn of the century and the 1960s. The editors welcome suggests for reprints. To receive our catalog or make suggestions, write The Rue Morgue Press, P.O. Box 4119, Boulder, Colorado (1-800-699-6214).

Catalog of Rue Morgue Press titles
as of March 2004

Titles are listed by author. All books are quality trade paperbacks measuring 9 by 6 inches, usually with full-color covers and printed on paper designed not to yellow or deteriorate. These are permanent books.

Joanna Cannan. The books by this English writer are among our most popular titles. Modern reviewers favorably compared our two Cannan reprints with the best books of the Golden Age of detective fiction. "Worthy of being discussed in the same breath with an Agatha Christie or a Josephine Tey."—Sally Fellows, *Mystery News.* "First-rate Golden Age detection with a likeable detective, a complex and believable murderer, and a level of style and craft that bears comparison with Sayers, Allingham, and Marsh."—Jon L. Breen, *Ellery Queen's Mystery Magazine.* Set in the late 1930s in a village that was a fictionalized version of Oxfordshire, both titles feature young Scotland Yard inspector Guy Northeast. *They Rang Up the Police* (0-915230-27-5, $14.00) and *Death at The Dog* (0-915230-23-2, $14.00).

Glyn Carr. The author is really Showell Styles, one of the foremost English mountain climbers of his era as well as one of that sport's most celebrated historians. Carr turned to crime fiction when he realized that mountains provided a ideal setting for committing murders. The 15 books featuring Shakespearean actor Abercrombie "Filthy" Lewker are set on peaks scattered around the globe, although the author returned again and again to his favorite climbs in Wales, where his first mystery, published in 1951, *Death on Milestone Buttress* (0-915230-29-1, $14.00), is set. Lewker is a marvelous Falstaffian character whose exploits have been praised by such discerning critics as Jacques Barzun and Wendell Hertig Taylor in *A Catalogue of Crime.*

Torrey Chanslor. *Our First Murder* (0-915230-50-X, $14.95). When a headless corpse is discovered in a Manhattan theatrical lodging house, who better to call in than the Beagle sisters? Sixty-five-year-old Amanda employs good old East Biddicut common sense to run the agency, while her younger sister Lutie prowls the streets and nightclubs of 1940 Manhattan looking for clues. It's their first murder case since inheriting the Beagle Private Detective Agency from their older brother, but you'd never know the sisters had spent all of their lives knitting and tending to their garden in a small, sleepy upstate New York town. Lutie is a real charmer, who learned her craft by reading scores of lurid detective novels borrowed from the East Biddicut Circulating Library. With her younger cousin Marthy in tow, Lutie is totally at ease as she questions suspects and orders vintage champagne. Of course, if trouble pops up, there's always that pearl-handled revolver tucked away in her purse. *Our First Murder* is a charming hybrid of the private eye, traditional, and cozy mystery, written in 1940 by a woman who earned two Caldecott nominations for her illustrations of children's books. In *Our Second Murder* (0-915230-64-X, $14.95), the sisters look into the murder of a socialite who was strangled with a diamond necklace. Final book in series.

Clyde B. Clason. Clason has been praised not only for his elaborate plots and skillful use of the locked room gambit but also for his scholarship. He may be one of the few mystery authors—and no doubt the first—to provide a full bibliography of his sources. *The Man from Tibet* (0-915230-17-8, $14.00) is one of his best (selected in 2001 in *The History of Mystery* as one of the 25 great amateur detective novels of all time) and highly recommended by the dean of locked room mystery scholars, Robert Adey, as "highly original." It's also one of the first popular novels to make use of Tibetan culture. *Murder Gone Minoan* (0-915230-60-7, $14.95) is set on a channel island off the coast of Southern California where a Greek department store magnate has recreated a Minoan palace.

Joan Coggin. *Who Killed the Curate?* Meet Lady Lupin Lorrimer Hastings, the young, lovely, scatterbrained and kindhearted daughter of an earl, now the newlywed wife of the vicar of St. Marks Parish in Glanville, Sussex. When it comes to matters clerical, she literally doesn't know Jews from Jesuits and she's hopelessly at sea at meetings of the Mothers' Union, Girl Guides, or Temperance Society, but she's determined to make husband Andrew proud of her—or, at least, not to embarrass him too badly. So when Andrew's curate is poisoned, Lady Lupin enlists the help of her old society pals, Duds and Tommy Lethbridge, as well as Andrew's nephew, a British secret service agent, to get at the truth. Lupin refuses to believe Diana Lloyd, the 38-year-old author of children's and detective stories, could have done the deed, and casts her net out over the other parishioners. All the suspects seem so nice, much more so than the victim, and Lupin announces she'll help the killer escape if only he or she confesses. Set at Christmas 1937 and first published in England in 1944, this is the first American appearance of *Who Killed the Curate?* "Marvelous."—*Deadly Pleasures*. "A complete delight."—*Reviewing the Evidence*. (0-915230-44-5, $14.00). The comic antics continue unabated in *The Mystery at Orchard House* (0-915230-54-2, $14.95), *Penelope Passes or Why Did She Die?* (0-915230-61-5, $14.95), and *Dancing with Death* (0-915230-62-3, $14.95), the fourth and final book in the series.

Manning Coles. The two English writers who collaborated as Coles are best known for those witty spy novels featuring Tommy Hambledon, but they also wrote four delightful—and funny—ghost novels. *The Far Traveller* (0-915230-35-6, $14.00) is a stand-alone novel in which a film company unknowingly hires the ghost of a long-dead German graf to play himself in a movie. "I laughed until I hurt. I liked it so much, I went back to page 1 and read it a second time."—Peggy Itzen, *Cozies, Capers & Crimes*. The other three books feature two cousins, one English, one American, and their spectral pet monkey who got a little drunk and tried to stop—futilely and fatally—a German advance outside a small French village during the 1870 Franco-Prussian War. Flash forward to the 1950s where this comic trio of friendly ghosts rematerialize to aid relatives in danger in *Brief Candles* (0-915230-24-0, 156 pages, $14.00), *Happy Returns* (0-915230-31-3, $14.00) and *Come and Go* (0-915230-34-8, $14.00).

Norbert Davis. There have been a lot of dogs in mystery fiction, from Baynard Kendrick's guide dog to Virginia Lanier's bloodhounds, but there's never been one quite like Carstairs. Doan, a short, chubby Los Angeles private eye, won Carstairs in a crap game, but there never is any question as to who the boss is in this relationship. Carstairs isn't just any Great Dane. He is so big that Doan figures he really ought to be considered another species. He scorns baby talk and belly rubs—unless administered by a pretty girl—and growls whenever Doan has a drink. His full name is Dougal's Laird Carstairs and as a sleuth he rarely barks up the wrong tree. He's down in Mexico with Doan, ostensibly to convince a missing fugitive that he would do well to stay put, in *The Mouse in the Mountain* (0-915230-41-0, $14.00), first published in 1943 and followed by two other Doan and Carstairs novels. A staff pick at The Sleuth of Baker Street in Toronto, Murder by the Book in Houston and The Poisoned Pen in Scottsdale. Four star review in *Romantic Times*. "A laugh a minute romp…hilarious dialogue and descriptions…utterly engaging, downright fun read…fetch this one! Highly recommended."—Michele A. Reed, *I Love a Mystery*. "Deft, charming…unique…one of my top ten all time favorite novels."—Ed Gorman, *Mystery Scene*. The second book, *Sally's in the Alley* (0-915230-46-1, $14.00), was equally well-received. *Publishers Weekly*: "Norbert Davis committed suicide in 1949, but his incomparable crime-fighting duo, Doan, the tippling private eye, and Carstairs, the huge and preternaturally clever Great Dane, march on in a re-release of the 1943 *Sally's in the Alley*. Doan's on a government-sponsored mission to find an ore deposit in the Mojave Desert…in an old-fashioned romp that matches its bloody crimes with belly laughs." The editor of *Mystery Scene* chimed in: "I love Craig Rice. Davis is her equal." "The funniest P.I. novel ever written."—*The Drood Review*. The raves continued for final book in the trilogy, *Oh, Murderer Mine* (0-915230-57-7, $14.00). "He touches the hardboiled markers but manages to run amok in a genre known for confinement. . .This book is just plain funny."—Ed Lin, *Forbes.com*.

Elizabeth Dean. In Emma Marsh Dean created one of the first independent female sleuths in the genre. Written in the screwball style of the 1930s, the Marsh books were described in a review in *Deadly Pleasures* by award-winning mystery writer Sujata Massey as a series that "froths over with the same effervescent humor as the best Hepburn-Grant films." *Murder is a Serious Business* (0-915230-28-3, $14.95), is set in a Boston antique store just as the Great Depression is drawing to a close. *Murder a Mile High* (0-915230-39-9, $14.00) moves to the Central City Opera House in the Colorado mountains, where Emma has been summoned by an old chum, the opera's reigning diva. Emma not only has to find a murderer, she may also have to catch a Nazi spy. "Fascinating."—*Romantic Times*.

Constance & Gwenyth Little. These two Australian-born sisters from New Jersey have developed almost a cult following among mystery readers. Critic Diane Plumley, writing in *Dastardly Deeds*, called their 21 mysteries "celluloid comedy written on paper." Each book, published between 1938 and 1953, was a stand-alone, but there was no mistaking a Little heroine. She hated housework, wasn't averse to a little gold-digging (so long as she called the shots), and couldn't help antagonizing cops and potential beaux. The result is one of the oddest mixtures in all of crime fiction. It's what might happen if P.G. Wodehouse and Cornell Woolrich had collaborated on a crime novel. The Rue Morgue Press intends to reprint all of their books. Currently available are: *The Black Thumb* (0-915230-48-8, $14.00), *The Black Coat* (0-915230-40-2, $14.00), *Black Corridors* (0-915230-33-X, $14.00), *The Black Gloves* (0-915230-20-8, $14.00), *Black-Headed Pins* (0-915230-25-9, $14.00), *The Black Honeymoon* (0-915230-21-6, $14.00), *The Black Paw* (0-915230-37-2, $14.00), *The Black Stocking* (0-915230-30-5, $14.00), *Great Black Kanba* (0-915230-22-4, $14.00), *The Grey Mist Murders* (0-915230-26-7, $14.00), *The Black Eye* (0-915230-45-3, $14.00), *The Black Shrouds* (0-915230-52-6, $14.00), *The Black Rustle* (0-915230-58-5, $14.00), *The Black Goatee* (0-915230-63-1, $14.00). and *The Black Piano* (0-915230-65-8).

Marlys Millhiser. Our only non-vintage mystery, *The Mirror* (0-915230-15-1, $17.95) is our all-time bestselling book, now in a seventh printing. How could you not be intrigued by a novel in which "you find the main character marrying her own grandfather and giving birth to her own mother," as one reviewer put it of this supernatural, time-travel (sort of) piece of wonderful make-believe set both in the mountains above Boulder, Colorado, at the turn of the century and in the city itself in 1978. Internet book services list scores of rave reviews from readers who often call it the "best book I've ever read." If ever a book could be called a modern classic, this one is it.

James Norman. The marvelously titled *Murder, Chop Chop* (0-915230-16-X, $13.00) is a wonderful example of the eccentric detective novel. "The book has the butter-wouldn't-melt-in-his-mouth cool of Rick in *Casablanca*."—*The Rocky Mountain News*. "Amuses the reader no end."—*Mystery News*. "This long out-of-print masterpiece is intricately plotted, full of eccentric characters and very humorous indeed. Highly recommended."—*Mysteries by Mail*. Meet Gimiendo Hernandez Quinto, a gigantic Mexican who once rode with Pancho Villa and who now trains *guerrilleros* for the Nationalist Chinese government when he isn't solving murders. At his side is a beautiful Eurasian known as

Mountain of Virtue, a woman as dangerous to men as she is irresistible. First published in 1942.

Sheila Pim. *Ellery Queen's Mystery Magazine* said of these wonderful Irish village mysteries that Pim "depicts with style and humor everyday life." *Booklist* said they were in "the best tradition of Agatha Christie." Beekeeper Edward Gildea uses his knowledge of bees and plants to good use in *A Hive of Suspects* (0-915230-38-0, $14.00). *Creeping Venom* (0-915230-42-9, $14.00) blends politics and religion into a deadly mixture. *A Brush with Death* (0-915230-49-6, $14.00) grafts a clever art scam onto the stem of a gardening mystery.

Craig Rice. *Home Sweet Homicide.* This marvelously funny and utterly charming tale (set in 1942 and first published in 1944) of three children who "help" their widowed mystery writer mother solve a real-life murder and nab a handsome cop boyfriend along the way made just about every list of the best mysteries for the first half of the 20th century, including the Haycraft-Queen Cornerstone list (probably the most prestigious honor roll in the history of crime fiction), James Sandoe's *Reader's Guide to Crime,* and Melvyn Barnes' *Murder in Print.* Rice was of course best known for her screwball mystery comedies featuring Chicago criminal attorney John J. Malone. *Home Sweet Homicide* is a delightful cozy mystery partially based on Rice's own home life. Rice, the first mystery writer to appear on the cover of *Time*, died in 1957 at the age of 49 (0-915230-53-4, $14.95).

Charlotte Murray Russell. Spinster sleuth Jane Amanda Edwards tangles with a murderer and Nazi spies in *The Message of the Mute Dog* (0-915230-43-7, $14.00), a culinary cozy set just before Pearl Harbor. "Perhaps the mother of today's cozy."—*The Mystery Reader*.

Sarsfield, Maureen. These two mysteries featuring Inspector Lane Parry of Scotland Yard are among our most popular books. Both are set in Sussex. *Murder at Shots Hall* (0-915230-55-8, $14.95) features Flikka Ashley, a thirtyish sculptor with a past she would prefer remain hidden. It was originally published as *Green December Fills the Graveyard* in 1945. Parry is back in Sussex, trapped by a blizzard at a country hotel where a war hero has been pushed out of a window to his death in *Murder at Beechlands* (0-915230-56-9, $14.95). First published in 1948 in England as *A Party for None* and in the U.S. as *A Party for Lawty*. The owner of Houston's Murder by the Book called these two books the best publications from The Rue Morgue Press.

Juanita Sheridan. Sheridan was one of the most colorful figures in the history of detective fiction, as you can see from the introduction to *The Chinese Chop* (0-915230-32-1, 155 pages, $14.00). Her books are equally colorful, as well as examples of how mysteries with female protagonists began changing after World War II. The postwar housing crunch finds Janice Cameron, newly arrived in New York City from Hawaii, without a place to live until she answers an ad for a roommate. It turns out the advertiser is an acquaintance from Hawaii, Lily Wu. First published in 1949, this ground-breaking book was the first of four to feature Lily and be told by her Watson, Janice, a first-time novelist. "Highly recommended."—*I Love a Mystery*. "Puts to lie the common misconception that strong, self-reliant, non-spinster-or-comic sleuths didn't appear on the scene until the 1970s."—*Ellery Queen's Mystery Magazine*. The first book in the series to be set in Hawaii is *The Kahuna Killer* (0-915230-47-X, $14.00). "Originally published five decades ago (though it doesn't feel like it), this detective story featuring charming Chinese sleuth Lily Wu has the friends and foster sisters investigating mysterious events—blood on an ancient altar, pagan rites, and the appearance of a kahuna (a witch doctor)—and the death of a sultry hula girl in 1950s Oahu."—*Publishers Weekly*. Third in the series is *The Mamo Murders* (0915230-51-8, $14.00), set on a Maui cattle ranch. The final book in the quartet, *The Waikiki Widow* (0-915230-59-3, $14.00) is set in Honolulu tea industry.